MOTHER RUSSIA

by

MERVYN MATTHEWS

MOTHER RUSSIA

by

MERVYN MATTHEWS

Hodgson Press

First published in Great Britain by Hodgson Press 2008

Hodgson Press
PO Box 903A
Kingston upon Thames
Surrey
KT1 9LY
United Kingdom

enquiries@hodgsonpress.co.uk

www.hodgsonpress.co.uk

Copyright © Mervyn Matthews, 2008

All rights reserved. No part of this publication may be reproduced, stored in a retrieval system, or transmitted, in any form, or by any means, without the prior permission in writing of Hodgson Press, or as expressly permitted by law, or under terms agreed with the appropriate reprographics rights organization. Enquiries concerning reproduction outside the scope of the above should be sent to Hodgson Press at the above address. Illustrations copyright of their copyright holders.

The moral right of the author has been asserted.

You must not circulate this book in any other binding or cover and you must impose this condition on any acquirer.

A CIP catalogue record for this book is available from the British Library.

ISBN: 978-1-906164-05-8

Printed in Great Britain by Lightning Source Ltd.

Typesetting and layout by Bernard Lowe

Contents

Acknowledgements

Chapter One

In which 'Mother Russia' acquires some
Interesting New Clients 1

Chapter Two

In which the local Council intervenes, and Ivan
Ivanich returns 31

Chapter Three

Mainly concerning a large fridge, fortune-telling,
and a fire 67

Chapter Four

In which we observe amorous endeavours, albeit
senile: the fridge losing part of its contents; and
an unusual gathering in a grave-yard 99

Chapter Five

Olga meets an old friend, the Russian Orthodox
church intrudes, and Trevor gets unusual
employment 131

Chapter Six

A ladies' day at the beach, disturbing news, and
a visit to a police station 163

Chapter Seven

Another chapel visit: two elderly spinsters spring
their trap, and more astonishing events occur at
'Mother Russia' 195

Epilogue

All loose ends tied up 235

Acknowledgements

A particular word of thanks is due to my good friends David Holohan and Berni Lowe for many useful suggestions, on-going encouragement, and a great deal of technical advice.

Mervyn Matthews

July 2008

MOTHER RUSSIA

Chapter One

(In which 'Mother Russia' acquires some Interesting New Clients)

It was early evening in Swansea. Trevor Jenkins strode purposefully down High Street, his umbrella angled carefully against the driving rain. His raincoat, despite the heavenward protection, was half-soaked, and he could feel a trickle of wet between his toes. "Typical summer weather," he muttered under his breath. "Heavy rain and a gale with it. I should have come in the car, but there's nowhere to park. Still, I've got more important things to think of, haven't I?"

Trevor was not, at first sight, a particularly heroic figure, such as might play an exciting role in a dangerous adventure. Though in a good age-group - his early thirties - he was perhaps a little too thin, a little too tall, and not very assertive. But he was obviously a friendly type, quick to smile, and his blue eyes had a sincere look about them. The only unusual thing about his physical appearance was his 1930s hairstyle: he insisted on parting his light brown thatch in the middle, as his father might have done half a century before. Indeed, his mother, before she died, was uncomfortable about it: where had he got that idea from? Did it betoken a hidden, untoward individuality which was not apparent in his daily behaviour? It was not, as she once intimated, the sort of chevelure which would attract a nice, steady girl-friend. Trevor, though on the look-out, like most young men of his age, had not found a partner among the eager Swansea womanhood who milled about him. In the absence of one, he indulged in a number of less exciting hobbies (including bottle collecting, table-tennis, rambling, with a bit of local history thrown in.)

2   *Mother Russia*

So far, moreover, Trevor had experienced very little in the way of adventure. His degree in Geography from Singleton College, though third class, might well have served as a basis for travel and adventure, but that was not to be. After an uncomfortable period of unemployment (he disliked being kept by his ageing mother in their two-bedroom house in the Hafod) he had found a specific demand for his geographical skills: Swansea Sewers Ltd., a splendid local company, was up-grading its out-of-date maps of these essential waterways and was looking for assistance. The firm had found difficulty in getting anyone to take the job, as a certain amount of distasteful subterranean wading was involved: but Trevor saw their advertisement and, albeit reluctantly, applied. He turned out to be just the sort of person they wanted – Swansea-born, knowledgeable about the lay-out of the streets, apparently reliable, and, most important of all, ready to start immediately.

Unfortunately the job only lasted a few weeks, following an unfortunate incident under a road surface, to be recounted later. So on that wet evening in High Street, Trevor was again without full-time employment. He felt, however, that things might again be moving in the right direction. "Yes," he said to himself. "Change is afoot. I can't go sewering again and there's no other geographical work in sight. Mother's dead and gone – there's no one in the house but me and the cat. But now I'm a free agent all around. And the inheritance..." He paused as the figures – not very impressive - flashed through his mind. "I hope I'm doing the right thing by putting a few thousand into this Mother Russia eating house thing. Olga seems to be managing all right. I wonder how she's getting on with the week's accounts at the moment? She should have them ready by the time I get there."

At this point he turned into Salubrious Passage, a narrow alleyway off Wind Street, and paused before a

Chapter One 3

modest façade which had been altered by a false log arrangement to create the impression of a Russian peasant hut with a rustic portal. The premises behind were obviously converted from the sort of two-bedroom terraced house Trevor had been born and grew up in. A plywood sign representing a balalaika hung above the doorway, and a portly life-size wooden doll, a Russian matryoshka, stood on castors on the pavement outside. A sign with "Mother Russia – Swansea's only Russian Restaurant," written in what Trevor imagined to be Russianized lettering, graced a little window, onion-shaped, in the main door. An old-fashioned brass knob protruded from the door frame, looking as though it was waiting to be pulled.

"The place looks quite exotic," he thought, approvingly. "I'm sure there's never been anything like it in the town before. If only we can advertise it properly, it could go like a bomb."

Although the Russian eatery was his destination, Trevor walked past the entrance and approached a small side-window. Glancing around to make sure that there were no curious onlookers, he peered in through the heavy lace curtains. A fan-light was open, and he could just hear a woman's voice inside, low and accented. His expression, hitherto a little tense, softened. It was Olga counting the takings. He could just make her out through the frills.

"Now let me see," said the voice. "Not very good takings again this week, is it? Forty eight dinners with rabbit and beetroot soup, and Rostov rissoles, at three pounds fifty a dinner, total.... one hundred and sixty-eight pounds. Twenty-three vodka breakfasts at four pounds a time ... ninety-two pounds ... Trevor heard her pause, evidently to note some figures. "My dear little restaurant," she exclaimed. "Mother Russia, how can we find more customers and fill their bellies with good Russian food?

4 *Mother Russia*

To make just a little profit. The people here just don't know what they're missing..."

Trevor tapped on the window and Olga looked up. He pressed his nose hard against the glass.

"Hello, it's m-ee-e. All ready for another evening's work!"

"Oh, Trevor my little darling" said Olga, rising quickly from behind the desk and approaching the window. "What a funny little nose you have when it's flat. I'll open the door for you. It's not seven yet. I'm just doing the accounts! You always come early, not like these Russians."[1]

She bounced out of the office, and a moment later the door was opened by an amply proportioned female, with pleasant, rather swarthy features, indicating perhaps some Tartar provenance. Her grey-blue eyes were wide with pleasure. She was evidently a year or two younger than Trevor, and still undeniably attractive. For some males, an excessive use of make-up might have detracted from the overall positive impression, but Trevor had by now got used to it. She was attired in a peasant costume – a heavy, brightly embroidered dress with white sleeves. A traditional Russian tiara graced her bottled-blond locks. As soon as Trevor crossed the threshold she threw herself upon him: though not unpleasant, he thought, it was like being attacked by a feather bed. Trevor had never quite made up his mind about Olga since meeting her a few weeks before (when he first happened to have lunch at the restaurant.) She was obviously warm and soulful, but not quite his type.

---

[1] Adequate representation of inimitable Russian accents in English lettering has proved well-nigh impossible, apart from being difficult to read. So the author has largely abandoned the attempt, leaving the transmogrification to his readers' imagination. Most of the Russian speech has also been translated into 'normal' English to avoid incomprehension and distress.

Chapter One **5**

"Come in to our little office," she said. "You look a little bit sleepy, Trevushka. Didn't you sleep well last night? Didn't you dream of your little Olga? But you're all wet, too! And your feet! Take off your mac and your shoes. Put these nice dry slippers on instead."

She took his coat and handed him a pair of plaited peasant slippers before leading him into a tiny room under a stairway. Trevor had been there several times already: the contents were a strange mixture of past and present – a battered, though obviously ancient, icon with a little lamp hanging in one of the corners, a sagging red sofa which looked as though it had also made a journey from distant parts, while a modern, though obsolescent, computer and a filing cabinet completed the furnishings. It was all concealed from curious eyes by the lace curtains.

"Here we are again, Trevushka. Sit down on the sofa – it came all the way from Russia, like me. Rest your sleepy head on my lovely Russian bosom. I like you when you're sleepy."

"Oh dear, Olga, "said Trevor, with a little laugh. "Not just now... You're in the middle of the accounts, I see." (She's got lovely big tits, he thought, but business is business.)

"Bugger the accounts, darling! I want to be close to you."

"Olga, you mustn't say words like 'bugger'. Where did you learn that? It's rude. Cosy in here, though, isn't it? You're right, I didn't get much sleep last night. My stomach was upset. I think it was the rabbit soup that done it. What did they put in it?"

"Lovely fresh rabbits from the Welsh hills, darling. In Russia it's called borsch, that's because it has beetroot in it as well. Sit down close to me and let me massage your little belly... Some of the Russian dishes are too strong for

6   *Mother Russia*

you. Just you trust Auntie Dasha and Auntie Masha in the kitchen. They are very careful about what they give you to eat. Perhaps it was the Russian video you watched with me yesterday evening, before you went home."

"Oh no, Olga! It was definitely the food. Mind, that *Ivan the Terrible* video was enough to upset anyone. I mean, all of those peasants having their balls twisted and their throats cut! It was gruesome!"

"I chose it special for you. It's only when you see a real film about Russia you know how lucky you are to live here in Swansea. Especially if you can settle down with a nice girl who will love you passionate all your life long." The springs of the divan twanged as she edged herself closer to him.

"Olga. Ger-roff," he cried, though somewhat reluctantly. "You'll break the sofa. It isn't very strong. And your aunties will be out of the kitchen in a minute... Now what about the takings? Don't forget, I've invested some of my inheritance in this. Two thousand pounds. It's a lot of money, especially if you're unemployed."

"Of course I know, darling. Without you, we couldn't carry on. But you never told me how you lost your job."

"Oh Olga," said Trevor, trying without success to catch a glimpse of the figures on the desk. "I want to know how we are getting on.... our business is far more important ... Oh, all right then, I'll tell you. But after that we must discuss the takings. Okay?"

"Okay, darling," said Olga. "Tell me first, then we'll discuss the figures."

"You know I worked with Swansea Sewers until I had my accident."

"What's 'sewers'? I don't know that word."

Chapter One   **7**

"Drains and all that. Sanitation. Where all the stuff goes from lavatories and sinks. My job was to check the old sewer maps, because the sewers had been altered many times, and the maps were muddled up. I had to go through the old tunnels and check them against the maps. It was a terrible job, even if you like maps. But I couldn't find anything else. I had only been at it a few weeks when I was traumatised."

"Who?"

"Sorry Olga, you can't know those hard words. I had a nasty accident."

"What was that?"

"One day, when I was working in the Grand Victoria, a rat got up my trouser leg, and before I could do anything about it, it bit my bum. I nearly went berserk. The Grand Victoria is the big tunnel under Prior Street, named after the great British queen. I was writhing and twisting something terrible. My mates had a terrible job getting me up through the manhole." Trevor smiled shyly. "A crowd gathered to watch. Was I embarrassed!"

"Oh, my God," said Olga. "Worse the *Ivan the Terrible*. So what happened after that?"

"They managed to stun it with a brick through my trousers, but they were afraid I might have blood poisoning. So they got an ambulance, but the rat came to and ran down my trouser leg and bit the ambulance man. As a matter of fact, all the commotion stopped the traffic. Then they took me to hospital to get my bum dressed. It's still not quite right."

"Let Olga see it and rub it better," said she immediately. "I got some lovely bear grease that they use in Siberia. It don't smell very nice, but you get used to it. Pull your trousers down."

8   *Mother Russia*

She jumped up and went to a shelf under the icon, where stood a little jar topped with grease-proof paper. As she opened it and turned towards him, Trevor giggled.

"No, Olga, no bear grease," he said. "It happened weeks ago, and it's nearly healed now... We don't do that sort of thing here, you know. Especially in the office."

"Go on," said Olga, imperiously. "Let me see it!"

"*No*, Olga!"

Resigned to failure, she put the jar back on the shelf.

"So when they got me to hospital, a psychiatrist said that after an incident like that, I could develop claustrophobia and go mad underground, and that I was never to go down a sewer again. So I lost my job just out of the blue."

"What's 'out of the blue'? Trevushka? I never heard that either."

"Something unexpected, Olga," he explained with a sigh. "But I've got a feeling that things will change. If I can get myself into psycho-analysis on the National Health and get a decent job with geography it would be wonderful. I always have such a feeling of... well, fulfilment, with maps and things. But what about Mother Russia? Tell me how much we've taken this week. I know it's been quiet."

Olga appeared not to hear him, and in an instant had pulled him back down onto the sofa. She leaned over him and looked softly into his eyes, confirming his earlier impression that she used too much mascara.

"Do you love me, darling, just a little beet?" Her lips advanced closer.

"Too much lipstick, as well," he thought. "We've only known one another for three weeks, Olga," Trevor gasped. Things don't move that fast around here. How can I love

Chapter One   **9**

you after so short a time?" Olga pouted and kissed him on the tip of his nose.

"Yes you do, my sweet little goat."

"Is that what they call people in Russia? I've never heard of anyone calling their boyfriend a goat in Swansea. Of course, I quite like you Olga. You've got sterling qualities."

"Oh no I haven't," Olga replied quickly. "None of us have got any money at all. That's why we are so grateful for your help. All I can give you is my warm love. Rest your little 'ed on my big soft bosoms."

"Oh, Gawd!" Trevor thought to himself. "There's no end to it, is there?"

"Bosom, Olga. Bosom," he said aloud. "In English women, have only got one. But I don't want to put my head anywhere. We're supposed to be checking the accounts."

She was still holding him down firmly.

"Poor Trevushka, what a lovely soul you have. In Russia we love people who have lovely souls. If the soul is clear, as the old saying goes, your parsnips will not dry out..."

"What have parsnips got to do with it?" he asked, genuinely puzzled. "But we've all got our problems. I haven't even got a proper job, except helping part-time in your kitchen."

There was a short silence as Trevor wondered how he could best get the conversation back to the accounts. He shook himself free and sat up. Olga, realising that his questions could be avoided no longer, took some papers from the table. They looked at one another.

"So, what were the takings this week?"

Olga began to sob.

10   *Mother Russia*

"Oh, Trevor! It's bad. The vodka breakfasts haven't caught on, not like in Russia. The people in Swansea don't start boozing till midday. And they aren't used to the Russian food. We just aren't getting enough customers. I'm afraid the bank will demand its loan back. And me and my aunties 'ave only got temporary visas, you know. The immigration may send us all back to Verkhoyansk when the visas finish next month. Just like that!" She made a sweeping farewell gesture, waving both her hands. "If only we could find husbands ere, any of us. That would be the best way out. At least, then they couldn't deport us, and we could stay here forever."

"People don't get hitched just like that, you know, Olga, just so that they can get visas. It's called a *marriage de convenance* in French, – a marriage of convenience. But I'll keep my ears open and if I hear of anyone who wants to marry a Russian aunty or two, I'll tell you. There's a club with a lot of randy old codgers in Briton Ferry, I've heard. They might fancy a bit of Russian petticoat. You shouldn't have much trouble yourself, though, you're only twenty-nine."

"Twenty-eight and some months," said Olga quickly. "But won't you EVER understand, Trevushka? YOU are the man of my dreams. YOU could be my support in life."

Trevor changed the subject back to business again.

"We'll have to do something to pull the customers in, Olga. I don't think this rabbit soup has caught on, especially with beetroot. People don't eat much beetroot in Wales. Leeks are the things here. I think some people have had stomach upsets from it already. A woman I know in the Hafod had lunch here last week, and she came to the house to complain."

"Well, we haven't had many complaints here," said Olga stoutly. "Well, only five or six... But I had another idea, Trev. Perhaps we could name the restaurant after a holy

Chapter One **11**

Russian saint, and call on him to help." She crossed herself, Orthodox fashion, and looked up at the icon.

"Is that the way Russians cross themselves, Olga? I didn't know you were religious. So you want divine intervention, call God in to help? I don't think it would make much difference. What saints are there, anyway? You need someone with a catchy Russian name, so you can put it on a sign, or in adverts."

"My grandmother taught me all about the saints when I was little. Saint Evdokia might do, she was a famous cook who lived many years ago. She worked as the cooking nun for Patriarch Tikhon. In his personal kitchen."

"Oh, Olg, you are clever. Evdo what?"

"'Evdokia'. He was so pleased with 'er borsch and cat pies," Olga continued, "that he got her made into a saint after she died. The cat pies caught on and there wasn't a cat left for miles around."

"I don't think that that sort of saint would mean much around here. And cat pies! What if people found out! Most people like cats around here. No one could pronounce the name, anyway."

"But there are many others."

"Who, for example?"

"Saint Sergei Velikobriukhin. 'E's the patron saint of all Russians who eat too much."

"We call them gluttons, Olg."

"The Saint of Russian... gluttons, then. In the end 'e died of over-eating. How you think that sounds? *Velikobryukhin.*"

"Gosh! That's good, but no one could pronounce that either. Does it mean anything?"

12   *Mother Russia*

"Let me think... Velikobryukhin...   Velikobryukhin means having a big belly. Bigbelly! Saint Bigbelly. How does that sound? He might do a miracle on us..." She sighed again. "I never thought it would be as hard as this to run a restaurant in little Wales after I left Verkhoyansk. I'm bloody glad I did, though. Life here is much more exciting."

"Well, perhaps a picture of a Russian monk with a huge paunch might look nice..."

Olga was just about to ask him what a paunch was, when the sound of women screaming in the kitchen distracted their attention.

"*Gospodi pomilui... perestan' seichas zhe...*" The sound of great metal clangs, bongs, and a heavy thwack reached the little office.

Olga jumped up. "My God!" she said. "That's Masha and Dasha fighting again... with the saucepans. Every day they turn the kitchen into a bloody battle field. We must tell them. Quick!"

She jumped up and, closely followed by Trevor, she rushed through the dining room to a swing door which opened directly into the kitchen. It was a rather malodorous area, mainly on account of piles of stale vegetables, a large, open jar of pickled gherkins, and a quantity of rabbit entrails which hung from an over-filled garbage bin. The walls were stained with grease and God knows what else. Two large cauldrons of soup steamed on a gas stove which had seen better days, and was probably dangerous. There were frying pans full of half-cooked rissoles and flat noodles.

Two diminutive old crones, obviously twins, silver-haired and both with buns, dressed in stained white aprons, were engaged in their own variant of hand-to-hand combat, the nastiest they could manage in their

Chapter One **13**

declining years. In fact they were trying to hit one another, wherever possible, with heavy saucepans.

"Stop it!" screamed Olga. "You'll break the bloody saucepans. We haven't got money for new ones!"

She grabbed the nearest of the two, Auntie Dasha, by the neck from behind, and, with surprising agility, thrust her knee in the small of her back. Auntie Masha promptly took advantage of the situation and bonked her sister with one of the saucepans. Olga's tiara was knocked askew in the struggle, but Trevor managed to get hold of Auntie Masha from behind.

"Grab her as well," said Olga, panting with effort. "They can't help it. They've been quarrelling all their lives... They love it. They haven't got used to one another yet. So what's it this time?" she asked, when the two were finally separated.

"She got the false teeth, the old hag!" cried Dasha, relaxing a little at last. And she won't give them up. It's Thursday. They're mine on Thursdays. I'll kill her."

"Oh God," thought Trevor. "What a thing to fight over. False teeth!"

"Don't you call me an old hag, you old hag," Masha responded. "We're twins."

"Give - me – *my - false - teeth* - back, I say! You had them an extra day last week, too."

"I needed them today because kind old Mr. Thomas asked me out for a beer. I thought he might ask me to marry him, especially if he got drunk. You can't expect a good-looking man like that to propose to a lady with no teeth in her head, can you?"

"Well, anyway, he didn't ask you, did he? He's got too much sense."

14   *Mother Russia*

"You shouldn't have taken your balalaika when you went to see him, Auntie Dasha," said Olga, soothingly. "Probably that's what put him off. He was ashamed to see you playing it in public."

"Never mind the bloody balalaika," cried Dasha. "I want my teeth! Let's have them!" Somehow she managed to struggle free and again tried to bang her sister with the saucepan, which she had not relinquished. "Take that!" Fortunately, this time she missed.

"Come on girls," said Trevor in persuasive tones. "Break it up! We're opening in a few minutes. Why can't one of you get another pair from the dentist, on the National Health? You just go along, they measure your mouth, and you get a brand new set in a week."

"And you don't pay anything, either, Auntie Dasha," Olga added, "if you're old. They don't expect people to share false teeth in this country, you know."

"How can we go to the dentist if our visas are running out?" asked Masha. "We're not registered. They'll put us in prison, or send us back to Russia." A trace of fear passed across her lined face. For a moment Trevor felt a little sorry for her.

"They are rather lost, here," he thought. "And they aren't doing any harm!"

"They really ought to put you in prison," said Olga, with a show of indignation. "To teach you a lesson for quarrelling all the time. Okay, Auntie Masha, take them out."

Masha reluctantly poked a bony finger into her mouth and hooked out a pair of dentures.

"Ugh... That's right!" said Olga, peering at them. "Come over to the sink and hold them under the tap for a minute, they've got bits of pickled gherkin in them. Then

Chapter One **15**

give them to Auntie Dasha... That's better, feel all right, do they, Auntie?"

Auntie Dasha slipped them in and produced a triumphant, toothy smile.

"I've never heard of anyone sharing false teeth," said Trevor. "They do it in Russia, do they?"

"Only if they fit," said Olga disdainfully. "The Russians are very choosey, you know. This set must be getting a bit worn, though. They've been in the family for many years. They was my granddad's. He had them made after he got into a brawl with Rasputin, who knocked his front teeth out for him. You've heard of Rasputin, haven't you?"

Trevor nodded his head in agreement. He had, in fact, once read about Rasputin. The sorrowful monk was close to the Royal Family, and was 'very strong', which was the upper class way of saying that he possessed one of the sturdiest organs in Russia. But this, thought Trevor, was no moment to discuss a dead monk's anatomy.

He glanced around the kitchen: the two aunties were still panting from their exertions.

"My God!" he thought. "I didn't know what I was taking on when I teamed up with Olga. I hope she doesn't produce any more relatives like this."

"Okay, girls," he said aloud. "We can forget about teeth now. There's a bigger problem with the food. As I was telling Olga, a woman came to see me yesterday and complained about being sick after the rabbit borsch. She happens to be the district nurse and knows me. In fact, I felt a bit queasy myself after that borsch. Can you remember what you put in it? We haven't got enough customers as it is. No point in driving them off with upset stomachs."

Auntie Masha gave her sister a piercing glance.

16 *Mother Russia*

"It's your bloody fault, again, Dasha," she said. "You shouldn't have put Petya in it."

"What's 'petya'?" said Trevor, under the impression that it was a Russian herb.

"She means Peter the cat," Olga explained. "I thought it might cause trouble. He was ill with something."

Trevor felt queasy again, and glanced at the bucket of entrails. His question was superfluous, for a black tail of obvious feline provenance was hanging out of it.

"Jesus, Olga! They didn't boil the cat, did they?"

"They ate a lot of cat in Russia during the famine," said Olga defensively. "When everything else was finished, you ate the cat. Cat pies, cat stew, and roast-cat dinners. After the war, there wasn't a cat to be seen for hundreds of miles." She paused. "Lots of rats and mice, though."

Auntie Masha had started another emotional outburst.

"My lovely Petya," she wailed. "My dear little pussy! Gone for ever! How could she do it?" Then she turned vengefully on Dasha: "You're as blind as a bat without the glasses. You've lost them again, haven't you? Or were you drunk?" She looked around for a saucepan, but Trevor had prudently put them out of reach.

"Masha, please don't tell lies about me all the time," said Dasha, in her most dignified tone. "I am NOT blind and I was NOT drunk. I had to use the cat, because there wasn't enough rabbit."

"Hell's bells," thought Trevor.

"Apart from that, poor Petya 'ad been ill for weeks, and not eating. So I thought it would be a good thing to put him out of his misery."

Masha managed to lay a hand on another utensil, a frying pan this time, which was lying on the stove, and

Chapter One **17**

landed a glancing blow on her sister's shoulder. "Why you ..! Take that!"

"Stop it!" Olga screamed again, and the two ladies did indeed separate. "Didn't the poacher bring enough rabbits?"

"The poacher?" said Trevor. "Olga, what have they been up to?"

"He's the big man with a squint," Olga explained. "You may have seen him. He lets us have them cheap."

"Well, he didn't have enough," Dasha continued. "That's why I had to use Petya."

"I think she got some of him on the icon," said Trevor, glancing at the holy image which hung on the wall behind the chopping board. "I was wondering what those black bits were. It's cat fur... all stuck. They'll have to be washed off."

"Isn't it just dirt?" asked Olga, peering at the blobs closely.

"Well, it's Dasha's fault," said Masha. "She shouldn't clean things so close to a holy image."

"No, it's your fault, Olga," said Dasha reproachfully. "You shouldn't have hung it so low. And I can't see very well without the glasses. Where are they, anyway?" Her question, however, remained unanswered, as Olga extracted an antique silver watch from a secret pocket in her cleavage. "It's nearly opening time," she announced. "Trevor, can you get your Russian costume on?"

With the latest kitchen drama over, Trevor retreated to the office and pulled a large cardboard box out from under the sofa. It contained his Russian peasant outfit, to match Olga's: a loose white shirt with an embroidered neckline, to be belted over bright blue sharovari (loose-fitting Caucasian trousers); soft wickerwork slippers with

18   *Mother Russia*

tapes to be tied criss-cross over the calves, and a shapeless felt hat. Reluctantly, he began to put it all on: he always felt ridiculous in it. Surely Russian peasants hadn't dressed like that? But he had decided that if the costume attracted custom, he would wear it. He hoped that none of the people he had known at Swansea Sewers Ltd., or anyone from the Hafod, would see him. So far, the district nurse was the only one, when she came in for lunch. She had given him a condescending smile.

When he finished changing he looked at himself in Olga's mirror. "You didn't reckon on having to wear this outfit when you came into the business, did you?" he asked himself. "If the business goes well, though, we'll be able to get someone else in, and I'll come here in a dark business suit... As the manager."

He went out into the dining room and switched on the lights, for it was already getting dark. The interior had been made to look like the inside of a peasant hut, or *izba*: the walls were painted to look like logs, the table-cloths had brightly embroidered edges – Russian-fashion – and some pictures of Siberian forests, reproductions of well-known nineteenth-century works, hung on the walls. A portrait of the last tsar occupied the place of honour over the till, and a large bear skin, with the head intact, lay on the floor in one corner.

Trevor heard voices in the Passage outside – some potential customers had appeared already. Through the little glass window in the door, Trevor could just make out a group looking at the framed menu outside. "Starting early this evening," he thought. "They don't usually come at seven sharp. Perhaps we'll have more custom."

He opened the door to find a family of four – two adults, two tousle-haired boys and a thickset, middle-aged man, possibly a foreigner, waiting for opening time.

Chapter One **19**

"Welcome to Mother Russia!" he said, with what sounded like a Russian accent. The two urchins looked at his costume and started to laugh. Trevor was irritated, but pretended not to notice.

"Do all Russians look like that, mum?" one of them asked.

"Only the peasants," said the Father. "It's their traditional costume."

"Daft, isn't it?"

"Would you like to sit by the window, or in that corner?" Trevor asked the family, when they we all inside.

"We'll have a table by the window, please," said the Father. "Gareth, David, over there! Go on!"

Trevor glanced around and found that the thick-set gent had chosen the table in a corner.

"Would you like to see the menu?" Trevor asked, the family when they were seated. "I can recommend the set meal. The main item is the rabbit borsch, all red, with beetroot, and lovely rissoles and potato to follow. Then Russian compote."

"You choose, Sid," said the mother. "I've never been in a place like this before. It's all Russian."

"The set dinner is this rabbit soup with beetroot and rissoles, said Sid. I don't think the kids would like it."

"Well, you should have thought about that before we came in," said the mother. "It was all up on the menu outside."

"They've got a good drinks list, though. Three kinds of vodka."

"I knew you'd go for that as soon as you saw it."

20 *Mother Russia*

"Oh, Mum! I've never had rabbit soup," Gareth broke in. "Can I have that please?"

"And me!" said David.

"We'll have the set dinner for four, please, with the rabbit and beetroot soup and rissoles," Sid told Trevor, who was waiting expectantly. "Menna, what shall we have to drink? The kids will want something, too, I suppose."

"I'll have a glass of cider. What will you have, boys? There's orangeade, lemonade, or mineral water."

"Orangeade! Orangeade!" the boys cried.

"I knew the little devils would go for the dearest drinks," said Sid. "I'll have the lager."

"Dear?" said his wife. "It's only half the price of your lager. It won't be your last glass, either. I hope the food will be all right."

"Oh, it's lovely," said Trevor. "This is the only place in Swansea where you can get it. A lot of people come here often." He finished scribbling the order in his pad and looked up to see Olga sweeping out of the kitchen.

"Look boys, it's a lady dressed like a Russian peasant," said their Mother.

"There's funny," said Gareth. "They both are."

Olga, however, was concerned with other things. Picking up a menu from the counter, she hastened to the corner where the solitary diner was sitting, but on seeing him at close quarters she stopped in her tracks. She looked around, as though hesitating: Trevor, who had not yet left the dining room, caught the expression of fear in her eyes. He had never seen her look like that before. The diner looked up: it was obvious to Trevor that they had recognised one another. "I wonder what's going on there?" he thought.

Chapter One **21**

Trevor looked at the man more closely. He was tall, muscular, and dressed in a grey suit: he had high cheekbones, icy blue eyes, and there was the hint of a scar across his right cheek. It was a typically Slav face. His hair was plentiful, but greying.

"Not a very pleasant character," thought Trevor. "I wonder how Olga knows him?" He tried to listen, but found they were speaking Russian. It was clear that the guest was not only ordering dinner, for after a few words he and Olga started discussing something earnestly. Olga sat down on the edge of a chair for a moment, order book in hand. The Russian was making some sort of proposition, but there was an imperious note in his speech also. At last Olga took the order and retired to the kitchen, clearly flustered. Trevor followed her.

"Olga," he asked. "Who's that? Do you know him? He's Russian, is he?"

"Oh, Trevushka," she said, with a brave attempt at a smile. "It's Ivan Ivanovich Kravchenko from Verkhoyansk. What a coincidence!"

"You knew him in Russia, then?"

"A lot of people knew him in Russia. He was a well-known businessman."

"But you're afraid of him, aren't you?"

"Ah... no! I'm just a little bit shy! He was quite an important person in Verkhoyansk."

"Shy?" said Trevor. "You?... What's he doing in Swansea, anyway?"

"He's bought up a cockle business in Penclawdd," said Olga, serenely.

"Cockle business?" Trevor gasped. "A man from the middle of Russia? Impossible. It must be a cover for something. What was he asking you, then?"

Mother Russia

"Oh, not very much," Olga answered uneasily. "He wants to develop it. He suggested that we put cockles on the menu here."

"On the menu?" said Trevor, incredulous. "And laverbread, no doubt?"

"What's laverbread?"

"Boiled seaweed."

Olga's face assumed an expression of distaste.

"He says he's persuaded several restaurants to sell his cockles already," she said. "It could be very profitable. If it goes well he'll be importing caviar."

"It's obviously a crazy idea," said Trevor. "This isn't even a fish and chip shop. Believe you me, there must be more behind it."

"But it's natural that he should try a Russian place like this, isn't it?" said Olga. "Let's get on with things... the customers are waiting." She clearly wanted to change the subject.

As the old aunts put the orders together in the kitchen, Trevor tried to make sense of what he had just heard. This man Ivan looked a real thug, a Russian gangster, the last sort of client they needed. Perhaps Olga was not telling him everything?

"Why didn't you tell him we just couldn't do it?" he asked.

"Ivan Ivanovich doesn't like being refused," she replied.

The borsch was just about ready – they kept it simmering on the stove – so she and Trevor busied themselves with the service. It was clear to Trevor, however, that the Russian visitor had struck a disturbing note; Olga's mood, at first playful and flirty, had changed completely. He could ask her about it again later.

Chapter One **23**

"Here it is, boys," said Menna, when the borsch arrived. "My goodness, that was quick, wasn't it? You'd think they had it waiting behind the door. Gareth, now don't slurp." Cautiously, she tried some herself. "Oh, it's lovely," she said. "Isn't it, Sid?"

The boys took a spoonful each and looked at one another.

"Mam, I don't like this soup," said David. "It's all red and funny. I never had red soup before. And this white stuff floating in it tastes awful."

"That's sour *cream*," said Sid. "It's down on the menu. And we told you it was red."

"Yes," said Gareth. "David's right. It's terrible."

"I knew they wouldn't like it," said Menna.

"Well, they got to bloody well eat it now," said Sid. "I'm paying for it. The Russians make it like that, it's got lovely beetroot in it. Never mind the sour cream, boys, you can leave that. You can tell the boys you had borsch when you get back to school."

"Oh, Sid!" said Menna. "It's too foreign for them. We should never have come 'ere. I've never had soup with beetroot in it, neither. Nor sour cream. We should have gone to that nice pie shop by the market."

"I thought we'd try a new place," said Sid. "That's the trouble with you, Menna, no spirit of adventure. Jack Williams was 'ere and he said they puts a spoonful of vodka in everything."

"I knew it!" cried his wife. "You chose this place for the booze. That's the only spirit you think of! It's probably the only place in the country where they do it."

"The rissoles will be ready in a few minutes," said Trevor, who was observing reactions in the background.

Mother Russia

"I'm sure the boys will like them. In Russia the soup is always ready, but the rissoles have to be cooked fresh."

"Oh, look at the bearskin over there, boys," said Menna, in an attempt to interest them. "It's got a real bear's head, with great big fangs. How would you like to be bitten by those? Go and have a look at it until the rissoles come. But be quiet now, don't disturb that gentleman over there. And no rough games."

The boys slipped off their chairs and went over to examine it.

"I wonder what kind of bear it is," said David. "It must have been a polar bear."

"No way," said Gareth authoritatively. "Polar bears are white, stupid! This one was brown. It must have been a grizzly."

His brother, overwhelmed by the display of knowledge, knelt down and fingered the snout.

"I know," said Gareth, with a burst of inspiration. "I'll pull it over me and chase you. It'll be a good game."

"You'll never catch me!"

"You just watch!"

In an instant he had drawn the bearskin over his head, and they were both careering around the tables with yelps of excitement.

"Boys," cried their mother, "Stop it at once! Put that bloody rug back!"

"The little sods," exclaimed their father at the top of his voice. "Stop it!" The merriment, however, was not to be curtailed so easily. The youngsters were too absorbed to take any notice. Sid leaped up and darted after them. But disaster ensued.

Chapter One **25**

Gareth, looking behind him so as to escape his pursuers, barged into the table where the Russian was eating his borsch, and rocked it badly. The soup plate shifted, and though it was not actually upset, a good part of the contents slopped over the diner's lap. At that moment, Sid caught Gareth by the scruff of the neck, gave him a cuff, and sent him back to their table. Gareth was followed by a crestfallen David.

"Look what you've done now!" their Father shouted.

"I couldn't help it, dad. David was chasing me…"

Sid turned to the Russian's table.

"I'm sorry," he said.

The Russian, however, had jumped up, incandescent with rage. The front of his shirt, jacket, and trousers were soaked.

"Let me wipe it off," said Trevor quickly, flourishing a teacloth. Olga came out of the kitchen with the plates of rissoles, and on seeing what had happened, she put down her tray.

"Oh, Ivan Ivanovich!" she exclaimed. "I'm so sorry! Let Trevor wipe it off!" Trevor tried, unsuccessfully, to dab it, but Ivan Ivanovich was in no mood to be mollified.

"My best suit," he spluttered in heavily accented English. "The beetroot stains will never come out."

"He's right there," thought Trevor. "He can say goodbye to a few hundred quid."

"I'll get some hot water from the kitchen," said Olga. "I'm sure it will wash out."

"Don't bother!" said the Russian. "That would make me even wetter. I go home."

"We'll have it dry-cleaned for you, Ivan Ivanovich," said Olga, trying to sound accommodating. "And please have the meal at our expense."

"You no expect me to pay for it also?" said Ivan Ivanovich, with a nasty leer. He swallowed what was left of his glass of vodka. "I come and see you tomorrow."

In a moment he had grabbed his mac and was gone. The atmosphere in the dining room was suddenly subdued. Trevor started to clear the mess.

"Look what you've done now!" Menna whispered to Gareth tersely. "There's always something isn't there? Last week you had the arse out of your trousers."

"I haven't torn my clothes, mum, have I?" said David ingratiatingly. His brother gave him a terrible stare.

"Well shut up, and eat these bloody rissoles," said their Father.

Olga went over to their table.

"We've got some lovely dessert to follow," she said, invitingly. "Raspberry compote – stewed raspberries with cream. You'd like that, wouldn't you, boys? Then some Russian tea in a glass."

"Oh yes," said Menna. "They'd like that."

"And I'll have another bottle of beer," said Sid.

It was ten p.m., closing time. Olga was talking to the aunts in the kitchen, and Trevor was sweeping the dining room. It had been a very poor evening, even by Mother Russia's standards: apart from the two tables earlier, not a soul had crossed the quaint, rustic threshold.

"We'll really have to think of something new," Trevor said to himself. "Advertising? New dishes? Some gimmick.

Chapter One **27**

But obviously not cockles - and laverbread – that would be a laugh. A peculiar business with that Russian, to say the least. Olga said she knew him in Verkhoyansk... But what's he doing here? I wonder what's behind it?"

He reached the table where the Russian had been sitting and moved it slightly in order to sweep underneath. His broom suddenly caught an object on the floor – a smart, new briefcase. It obviously belonged to Ivan, because he was the only person to have sat at the table. Trevor had not noticed him carrying the case when he arrived, but he must have done so, and forgotten to take it when he left, angry and stained with beetroot. No doubt he would telephone, or call to collect it, in due course.

Trevor took the briefcase into the office, calling Olga as he did so. "Olga, your friend has left something."

She followed him in.

"He must have forgotten this when he rushed out," he said.

"He'll be back tomorrow," said Olga.

"He may not be sure where he left it," said Trevor.

They hesitated for a moment, exchanging glances.

"I wonder what's inside?" said Trevor. "He seems to be a pretty unsavoury type to me."

"Well, it really isn't our business," said Olga. "But we'll see what's in it anyway."

"Is it locked?" asked Trevor. "After all, there may be a telephone number or an address inside, so that we can contact him. We may be doing him a favour."

"We really should look."

"Well, we can't if it's locked," said Trevor. "Let's see."

28   *Mother Russia*

He put the briefcase on the desk and pressed the catch: it yielded. Without further ado Trevor opened the flap and they both peered inside. There were a few documents with local business headings and a copy of the Evening Post, the local newspaper. The paper seemed to have been folded so as to read an inside article. Trevor pulled it out and found that it was dated three days previously.

AFFRAY IN NEATH PUB

Last night the police were called in to The Gardener's Arms in Blackwell Place, Neath, to control a fight in which a number of people were involved. They were immigrants from Eastern Europe who had hired an upstairs room for a meeting. The police were tight-lipped, but a number of arrests were made, and four people were charged with disturbing the peace and causing an affray. Knives and razors were wielded, and three men needed treatment in hospital. None of the police officers were hurt.

The landlord of the establishment, Geoffrey Morris, is well known in the locality for his involvement in the "Keep Neath Clean" campaign. "They call themselves the Firebird Club, he told us, and they have been renting the room once a week for some months now. I think they're Russians and Ukrainians. I've no idea what goes on because it's all in Russian. They order a lot of vodka, but we haven't had any trouble before. An argument must have broken out among them. Most of the fighting was outside in the street, so there was no damage to the premises. We're not having them again, though. Enough is enough."

It is rumoured that the Ukrainian Mafia is trying to establish itself locally, and they are thought to be meeting opposition from a shady Russian gang. The police have charged certain persons with causing an affray.

Trevor and Olga looked at one another in silence.

Chapter One **29**

"Your Ivan may have been mixed up in it," said Trevor.

"Oh, my God!" said Olga. "I hope he doesn't get us involved. We've got enough problems already."

"What was he doing in Russia, then, when you knew him?"

"I knew OF him," said Olga. "He had a bad reputation as a local criminal. He'd been in prison several times. The police haven't arrested him here, though."

"Unless he's out on bail," said Trevor. "I think quite a lot of Russian criminals have come West since communism collapsed. Now let's see what else there is."

He carefully raised the edges of more papers, so as not to disturb the order. Most of them looked like business letters. Then he gasped. "Look at this," he said, as he got to the bottom. Olga peered into the depths of the briefcase as well.

"It's a razor."

"A razor," Olga repeated, weakly.

"Yes, and it's got some dried blood on it! Perhaps he's gone into hairdressing," Trevor added, with a trace of irony in his voice... "But something is obviously not right. A bloody razor in a briefcase! The only thing is, should we go to the police?"

"Oh, Trevor," said Olga, more emotional than he had ever seen her. "We can't do that! You know that our visas haven't been renewed. We could be deported for overstaying."

Trevor thought for a moment: this was definitely a dilemma. He'd never thought about visas, imagining that the residence problem was all fixed up. He had taken it for granted that the three women would have to attend to that themselves.

Mother Russia

"Well, you'll have to look into that," he said. "But it's another matter. As far as the briefcase is concerned, there's no reason why we should have looked inside or know anything about it. It's no business of ours. And we have no proof that the razor was used for anything illegal. Ivan could say he cut himself when he was shaving."

"If he found out that we went to the police," Olga added, "he'd certainly get at us."

"You're right, Olga," said Trevor. "So we'll sit tight and keep our mouths shut. The police are on to this Neath thing, anyway. You can tell me about the visa situation tomorrow."

Olga breathed a sigh of relief and looked at him gratefully. It was the first time he had observed any inkling of dependency in her. He squeezed her shoulder gently, in a brotherly fashion.

"Let's finish clearing up," he said. "Perhaps business will be better tomorrow."

Chapter Two

(In which the local Council intervenes, and Ivan Ivanich returns)

The old alarm clock in Trevor's bedroom rang shrilly, and its owner, roused from his slumbers, stretched out his arm and pressed the 'stop' lever. He preferred a clockwork appliance because, being a heavy sleeper, the battery-operated ones did not always wake him. He glanced at the dial to confirm that it was indeed ten past eight, his getting-up time since he lost his full-time job. He looked up at the ceiling with its two damp patches, and peeped over the bedclothes to check familiar light edging under the window curtain. If it was strong, the day was sunny: a dimmer glow betokened an overcast sky and more rain. "In days gone by," he thought sadly, "I would have been making my way along the Grand Victoria by now."

In fact, the past night had been a restless one, mainly because the problems at Mother Russia kept bumping against his subconscious. Had he done the right thing in putting all that money into it? Was it a viable business in the longer term? It was meeting Olga that tempted him. No emotional involvement, really, but she had a stunning personality... On the other hand, he saw no other prospect of employment for the time being. The sort of nine-to-five job that attracted most people was not for him: he wanted to be out and about, doing something active. True, the events of the previous evening had been exciting enough, with the bear-skin chase, the spilt soup, the razors and things, but that was not the kind of excitement he sought.

Mother Russia... His thoughts returned to Olga. "You get the impression," he reflected, "that she could make a

32   *Mother Russia*

success of anything. And so Russian. You wouldn't get a Welsh girl making the sort of suggestions that she does."

But as far as the restaurant was concerned, change – upgrading – was definitely needed, if the restaurant was to become a success. The kitchen, for one thing, had been allowed to get into a disgraceful state, what with the grease, the bucket of entrails, and two old women fighting over false teeth. That would have to be put right, and any more poisonings avoided. The menu was not attracting customers – was it a bit too exotic for the locality? Then – and a cold shiver ran down his spine under the blankets – there was that Ivan Kravchenko character. The man had not come back for his briefcase before the restaurant had closed, so he would certainly do so today. Of course, his idea of putting cockle dishes on the menu was absurd: but what lay behind it?

Trevor was on the point of getting up when the phone rang in the kitchen. He jumped out of bed and ran downstairs.

"Hello?"

"Trevor?"

It was Olga's voice.

"How are things?" he asked. He was a little surprised that she had phoned so early.

"Okay. But how are you this morning, my little goat?"

"Baa ..." said Trevor.

"Good news," she said. "Can you come in straight away?"

"What's happened?"

"A big order. I just had a telephone call from a Russian family in Treorchy." (She had, in fact, told him about them before: all the Russians in South Wales seemed to know one another.) "They want to organize a surprise birthday lunch for the granddad. The restaurant they booked earlier has let them down. I said we could do it."

"How many of them are there?"

"Nine or ten. For one o'clock. With balloons and decorations."

"I hope they won't get drunk and cause trouble."

"Not more that those Welsh children did last night."

"Okay, I'll be down in about half an hour. You haven't heard anything more from that Ivan, have you?"

"No. He probably doesn't have our phone number... But he'll be back."

Trevor put down the phone with some feeling of satisfaction. Perhaps business was looking up a bit, after all.

When Trevor arrived at the restaurant he found a notice "CLOSED FOR RECEPTION" pinned to the door. Inside, the place was transformed. Olga, Masha, and Dasha had created a festive air by hanging balloons from the side lights, while in the middle of the room four tables had been moved together to create a single festive board. An enormous floral teapot, the size of a small bucket, stood at one end. Antique cutlery, probably fake, had been set out, and bottles of vodka and Georgian wine stood invitingly at regular intervals. The serviettes had been set in heavy, ornate goblets, the best the restaurant could muster, while a few bowls of fruit and flowers added a rustic grace to the scene. Indeed, Olga and the two aunts were themselves admiring it as Trevor entered.

34   *Mother Russia*

"My goodness!" he said. "What a wonderful sight!" The old aunties simpered.

"In Russia," said Olga, "We always make a big effort for family celebrations. As the Russians say: You might be dead tomorrow. Then it will be too late."

"We say that as well," said Trevor. "I think everybody does."

"And you often are," cried Dasha.

"We all have our little tragedies, don't we?" said Olga. "Start doing the cold snacks, will you?" She ushered them into the kitchen.

"Trevor, my darling," she turned to him when they had gone. "How do you like the decorations?"

She tried to embrace him, but he stepped back.

"My God," he thought. "She's fast off the mark today, isn't she?

"Splendid," he answered. "I'm sure they'll be appreciated."

"And did you sleep well last night, and think of your little Olga?"

"Well, as a matter of fact, not very." He lowered his voice. "I was thinking about that briefcase and the razor. That Ivan fellow hasn't been back yet, has he?"

"No," said Olga, "Perhaps he won't come for days. The Russians are like that. Anyway, it's none of our business, is it? Just relax. Nothing's going to happen. Try and make a good impression on the people today – they're Russian, so they'll like the food. If we get known for family parties it could make a big difference to the business."

"Who's coming, then?"

Chapter Two **35**

"There's an old general from the Red Army who's visiting his daughter in Treorchy: it's his birthday. There's a sea captain, their wives, a few friends, and some little children. That's why we put the balloons up. The Russians love speeches, and there'll be a poet. But it could go on for hours. Get changed, my darling."

In fact Trevor had arrived none too soon – it was already well past twelve thirty. He had just finished donning his peasant costume when he heard voices in the street and the doorbell rang. He emerged from the office to see Olga admitting the party through the log entrance.

"Welcome, welcome!" she cried, with a broad smile. "My name is Olga! Come in! Everything is ready!"

A small crowd entered, led by a white-haired old man in a dark suit, his breast adorned with medals. He was evidently the main focus of the festivities. There was another old man, physically like him, perhaps a brother, similarly dressed, but without the medals; two or three ageing females, all blue-eyed, overdressed and overweight, no doubt wives and daughters; a bearded priest in Orthodox garb; a morose, skinny young man clutching a battered folder, immediately recognisable as a struggling poet; and three delightful little girls in white dresses, their hair gathered neatly in pigtails.

Olga bustled around as the guests chose their seats, with the general, his brother, and the oldest, matron-like woman at the head of the table, near the samovar. Thereupon, the two old aunties swept in with trays of *hors-d'oeuvres* – piles of black bread, plates of Russian salad, cold meats, pickled mushrooms, and horseradish sauce. Olga filled the small glasses with vodka, the goblets with wine, and the children's glasses with mineral water. Trevor observed it all with interest: it was all so much more elaborate than an English gathering would have been for the same sort of occasion.

36   *Mother Russia*

The young man with the folder rose to his feet. The conversation stopped, and everyone stared at him expectantly. He was, it seemed, the accepted master of ceremonies. The general looked down at his medals in sure anticipation of a deluge of compliments for his naval prowess.

"We have gathered in this admirable restaurant," said the young man, in nasal tones, "so aptly called Mother Russia, to pay our respects to Genadii Genadievich on his seventieth birthday. Olga Vasilievna Morozova and her staff have gone to great lengths to ensure a fine table." (Slight murmurs of approval ensued.) "To begin with, our children, the next generation, Natasha, Nadya, and Ksenia, have prepared their own little contribution, which you will hear in a minute. I have myself penned a brief ode, apposite (I hope) to the occasion. But first, Father Varfolomei will give us his blessing."

The priest rose to his feet slowly, in a manner befitting God's living representative. He cast a severe look over the assemblage and everyone bowed their heads.

"Lord God, bless this Orthodox table and all around it," he intoned. "May your spirit be among us on this auspicious day. May we be grateful for all your mercies, and the presence of Genadii Genadievich among us. God bless you all. Amen."

"Well, that was nice and short," Trevor murmured.

"Oh," said Olga. "The party will go on well into the afternoon, that's for certain. There'll be the toasts, speeches, and perhaps a sing-song. If we're lucky they'll run us out of vodka."

"Come on girls," said the master of ceremonies, beckoning to the shy little trio. "Come to the head of the table and sing your song." One of the women ushered

Chapter Two **37**

them up to their grandfather and hummed a note to start them off.

> "Happy Birthday to you.
> Happy Birthday to you.
> Happy Birthday dear Granddad.
> Happy Birthday to you,"

they sang. Then they each gave their grandfather a little posy, hitherto concealed behind their dresses. There was a little burst of applause and each child got a whiskery kiss from the old man.

Trevor, Olga and the aunts looked on approvingly.

"The Russian children are wonderful," said Olga. "So sweet!"

"Not like the little brats we had in yesterday," said Trevor. "Still, boys will be boys."

Attention now shifted back to the poet. He was on his feet again.

"I composed this little ode last week," he proclaimed, "after a walk around Penarth Docks. I know not what drew me there, no doubt the thought of the fine vessels which are moored there. But there is no finer hull, I thought, than the ship of Russia..." – he paused, so that his audience could applaud – "...which, though tossed on many a stormy sea, has come safely to port, steered by the steady hand of men like Genadii Genadievich. But first may I propose a toast to Genadii Genadievich, and congratulate him on a life-time of successful sea-faring."

The vodka glasses were seized with alacrity, and every adult, including the priest, downed an ample portion, Russian style, in one gulp. There were gasps of the traditional exclamation, "Bitter, bitter! But God forbid that this should be our last!" followed by forkfuls of *hors-*

38   *Mother Russia*

d'oeuvres. Olga went around the table filling the empty glasses in anticipation of the next libation.

"May I now read the ode?" said the poet, opening his folder. He cleared his throat and everybody looked at him expectantly. "Can you translate it for me as he goes," asked Trevor.

"My little darling wants to know the beautiful Russian poetry, does he?" said Olga. "Olga will try, but it will be hard."

The poet produced a torrent of verbiage, evidently a dramatic saga, waving is free arm and blinking dramatically. There were gasps of admiration from the diners. Even the little girls were transfixed.

"It's about a beautiful Russian naval boat," Olga explained to Trevor, "What do you say, a destroyer? At one time Genadii Genadievich was in command of a destroyer."

"Was he?" Trevor asked, but Olga did not have time to elaborate, the saga was moving too quickly.

"One dark night it crashed into a lighthouse in the Bristol Channel, and…

"Crashed into a lighthouse?" said Trevor incredulously.

"Sorry, crashed into the rocks around a lighthouse, because someone had forgotten to light it up. The ship sank, and all the sailors were thrown into the water. Genadii Genadievich, who was in the water among them, kept their spirits up with swigs of vodka from a bottle he had thoughtfully snatched from the ship's drink cabinet before it went down. Then the Penarth lifeboat came and rescued them. If it hadn't been for Genadii Genadievich's encouragement and foresight in getting the vodka, and his bravery, they would all have drowned…"

Chapter Two **39**

His ode finished, the poet sat down and reached for his goblet of wine. There was enthusiastic applause.

"The Penarth life boat?" Trevor asked Olga in amazement. "The lighthouse turned off? Drinking vodka in the Bristol Channel? What a load of cobblers! I don't believe a word of it. A Soviet destroyer could never get up there, anyway."

"Does it matter?" said Olga. "It must have happened or the poet wouldn't have written an ode about it, would he? It may have been a bit exaggerated, but that doesn't matter. It makes everyone feel good. Look at Genadii Genadievich!"

The old man was indeed beaming and thanking the poet volubly across the table. His red-faced companion arose, a little unsteadily.

"Oh, Viktor Viktorovich is going to make a speech now," said Olga. "I believe Genadii Genadievich's best friend. How lovely!"

"I hope it will be a bit more credible," said Trevor. "Can you translate if for me again, please?"

"I have known Genadii Genadievich for nearly fifty years," Viktor Viktorovich began, "and have never failed to be impressed by his intelligence, honesty, his devotion to duty, to his family..." – Genadii Genadievich's wife pressed a handkerchief to her eye – "...his personal reliability and bravery. All set off by a fine physique and handsome features."

("All the virtues," thought Trevor. "It must be a national characteristic. People here would cringe.")

"You all know the story from Genadii Genadievich's earlier years," the orator continued, "When he was working as a bosun on a Volga tug."

40 *Mother Russia*

("I suspect that's where he got to know Olga," thought Trevor.)

"The crew reckoned that someone, perhaps the cook, was cheating them of part of their vodka ration, and mutinied. They happened to be towing a caviar barge up to Nizhnii Novgorod."

"That's a town on the Volga," Olga explained.

"I know," said Trevor. "But you can't have a mutiny on a river. There's nowhere for the mutineers to escape to!"

"There is in Russia," said Olga. "We have very big rivers."

"And they don't ship caviar in barges, either. It's too small and precious."

"Genadii Genadievich confronted them single-handed," Viktor Viktorovich concluded triumphantly, and brought the tug safely to port. They were all arrested."

There was a round of applause, the vodka glasses were refilled with great rapidity. Olga looked on approvingly.

"Viktor Viktorovich was very brave," she said. "He worked on the tugs as well, but then he changed course and went into plumbing."

"Plumbing?" said Trevor.

"Yes, he was one of the best plumbers in Moscow, I'm told. He saved Russia millions of gallons of wasted water. The Russians are very careless about dripping taps, you know... They've got more important things to think about. But perhaps we should start serving the borsch. I'll get Masha and Dasha to help you to clear the plates. Top up the vodka and the wines, will you?"

Everybody was talking again and Trevor could see from the flushed faces that the alcohol was having an effect.

Chapter Two **41**

Genadii Genadievich was still more or less sober, but Viktor Viktorovich was distinctly drunk. A moment later, he rose unsteadily to his feet and asked to be directed to the gents: Trevor told him where it was, and thought no more of it. Olga appeared with a huge tureen of borsch. As she ladled it out, the diners busied themselves in passing around the black bread and sour cream, obligatory supplements to the soup. It was just at that moment that the door bell rang. Olga looked across at Trevor: Who could it be? There was a "Closed" notice up in the window. Two male figures could be distinguished behind the glass. Trevor hurried over and opened the door.

The men waiting outside had an official air: they were dressed in cheap suits, but clutched incongruously posh briefcases. The elder was in his forties, rather flabby, with thick glasses and an oversized trilby: the other was a decade or so younger, well-built, and undeniably handsome, with an engaging smile.

"Good afternoon," said Trevor. "I'm afraid the restaurant is closed to the public. There's a private party going on."

"Good afternoon," said the man in the trilby, in a deliberate, authoritative tone. "We will not, in fact, be dining. We have more important matters to attend to. I am..." – he paused, so as to give his words more weight – "... an Inspector of Environmental Health from the local council. My name is Algernon Alberthwaite."

He slowly removed his spectacles and, for greater effect, wiped them deliberately on his handkerchief. "We check commercial premises for cleanliness." (In fact, the idea that anyone should not know what an inspector of environmental health was had never crossed his mind.) "This is my assistant Mr. Earnest Whopp."

42   *Mother Russia*

Mr. Whopp grinned and gave a deferential nod.

"We wish to inspect the premises immediately," said Mr. Alberthwaite, "if not sooner."

"Could you call back later," said Trevor, in as off-handed a tone as he could manage. "As I said, we're in the middle of an important private function."

"No, sir! We cannot. We have been sent here as a matter of urgency."

By this time Olga had come up. She caught Mr. Alberthwaite's last remark and looked at Trevor uneasily. If there was anything the hard-pressed management of Mother Russia did not want, in the circumstances, it was busy-bodies from the council. Trevor was equally perturbed.

"Oh, my God!" he thought. "I wonder what's going to happen when they see the kitchen?"

The visitors edged their way into the dining room, Mr. Alberthwaite casting an officious glance at the festive arrangements: it was obvious that the inspectors were not going to be deterred. Fortunately, no one at the festive board took any notice of them.

"We would like to start with the kitchen," said Mr. Whopp. "I'm sure we won't disrupt anything going on here."

"Don't panic, Olga," Trevor hissed. "Everything will be all right. I know *all* about inspectors, we used to get them in the sewers."

"We had them on the tugs as well," said Olga.

At that moment, someone switched on the restaurant music system, and the sounds of "Black Eyes" filled the premises. Olga regained her composure, outwardly at least.

Chapter Two   **43**

"Well, if you must, gentlemen," she said, in ingratiating tones, "though it isn't very convenient. Welcome to our little corner of Russia. Perhaps you would like some nice rabbit borsch, our speciality? At one of the quiet side-tables. With just a spoonful of vodka to give it an extra something. Before you start."

"We will not be requiring any comestibles, thank you," said Mr. Alberthwaite in the same officious tone. "We're not supposed to accept benefactions from premises under investigation. And I was not aware that you had a drinks licence."

"We've applied for one," said Trevor quickly. "It has been approved."

"We only use a tiny little drop," said Olga, "to emphasise the Russian atmosphere. In the cooking. We don't need a drink licence, I'm sure."

"We will have to look into that further, madam," he added. "Mr. Whopp, could you make a note of that, please?"

Mr. Whopp opened his briefcase and pulled out a small dictating machine, into which he mumbled the necessary instructions. "Mother Russia... Check drinks licence." Then, with a little flourish, he put it back.

"Now, shall we get down to the inspection?" Mr. Alberthwaite continued. "Perhaps I should tell you a little more about why we are here. Following the five poison cases currently taking up half a ward at Swansea General Hospital, an investigation has been launched. It has been ascertained that all of the sufferers had had some rabbit soup at this restaurant."

"What a coincidence!" said Trevor.

"They were fresh rabbits from the Welsh 'ills," Olga added, somewhat incongruously.

44   *Mother Russia*

"I have therefore been instructed," Mr. Alberthwaite declared, as though he had not heard them, "to examine your premises as a matter of urgency. We can't have that sort of thing happening in a hygienic town like Swansea, you know. We've got an international image to maintain! We'll start with the kitchen, as Mr. Whopp suggested."

"Yes, the kitchen!" said Mr. Whopp, eagerly.

"Of course!" said Olga. "As long as it doesn't disrupt the service. But I would like to have just a little word with you in my office under the stairs first, Mr. er ... er ..."

"Al - ber - thwaite."

"Yes, of course, Mr. Albertwit. Please come this way." She cast a quick glance in Trevor's direction.

"Trevor, give Mr. Whopp a cup of tea in the kitchen, will you? You'd like that, Mr. Whopp, wouldn't you? Perhaps with some toast, and our wild strawberry jam! Mr. Albertwit and me will be along in a moment."

Mr. Whopp at first hesitated, but then decided that he should benefit, where possible, from the harmless perks of his trade. The confidential council instructions were to maintain good relations with the rate-payers, so as to facilitate inspection and, where possible, to get them to incriminate themselves. And it was only tea and toast.

"Just a quick cuppa, then," he said. "Is that all right, Mr. Alberthwaite?"

"Okay, but remember we're on duty. What would you wish to discuss in your office, madam?"

Olga, without answering, led the Inspector of Environmental Health past the festive table, where the guests had begun to sing along with the Russian tapes, and ushered him into her office, carefully closing the door behind them. She gesticulated to him to sit on the divan,

Chapter Two **45**

which he did somewhat hesitantly. Rather to his surprise, she sat down close beside him.

"What did you wish to discuss?" Mr. Alberthwaite repeated. "I should tell you that most of the rules covering these inspections are set out in council leaflets. Mr. Whopp has some in his briefcase. Nothing can be allowed to interfere with the inspection."

"There was a little thing I wanted to show you before you began," said Olga, in low, intimate tones. "I was trained for catering in the Russian River Fleet."

"Oh, were you?" said Mr. Alberthwaite.

"I have diplomas I can show you."

"I don't suppose they're relevant here. We have our own regulations, you know."

"But I would like you to see them," said Olga insistently, raising her bosom as close to Mr. Alberthwaite's face as the divan would allow. "There are two of them. They're exquisite."

"Well, I couldn't read them anyway, could I?" said Mr. Alberthwaite, trying both to look serious and ignore the partially revealed mammae. "They'd be in Russian, anyway."

"They've got my name written across them in gold letters."

Olga made a tiny adjustment to the cleft in her dress, and managed to get her breasts to quiver slightly. A good job that she had, with a strange premonition of need, sprayed herself with a cheap Russian perfume a little earlier.

"If you don't know Russian it doesn't matter, she continued affably. "Reading them is not all that important. You can admire them for what they are. And

46   *Mother Russia*

touch the parchment. The girls in the River Fleet catering section were green with envy."

Mr. Alberthwaite cleared his throat and blinked behind his lenses. "Normally we proceed straight to the kitchens, to see what's going on. With our own eyes. No hanky panky."

"What's hanky panky?" said Olga. "It's not on our menu. Mother Russia haven't got anything to hide. Sit closer to me on my little red divan. It came all the way from Russia... Like me."

"It's very kind of you, but I'm here on official business, Madam ...er.. Morozova."

"Just call me Olga, its friendlier. We Russians like to be friendly. And what was your first name, again?"

"Algernon," said Mr. Alberthwaite, softening a little. If she was a rate-payer, she should probably be humoured, he thought to himself. "My friends call me Algy. But I'm here on official business, you know. So at Mother Russia – I'm Mr. Alberthwaite."

"What a fine name... Algy...   Russian girls would like that. And easy to pronounce. I would like to say it every day!" She laughed.

Mr. Alberthwaite momentarily weighed his career prospects against Olga's offer of daily contact, and decided that the allure of the post of Deputy Head Environmental Officer, for which his name had gone forward, was too strong to risk. If the office found out that there had been any hanky panky...

"I'll not be examining your diplomas just now, madam," he said, straightening up a little. "With regard to the poisonings, the hospital laboratory says you appear to have developed a vicious brand of bacteria that local stomachs cannot tolerate... unless you brought it all the

Chapter Two **47**

way from Russia, like the sofa... and your diplomas." (He gave a dry little laugh.) "Ah-hm. Excuse me."

"Oh, Algy!" said Olga, feeling that she was losing the initiative. "I brought much more interesting things than bacteria... But regarding the kitchen, it's all very hygienic, my two aunts look after it. But please relax! There's plenty of time."

"No there isn't," said Mr. Alberthwaite. "We've got to do a fish and chip shop in Fforestfach this morning as well. They've been using it to market undersized cod. I can tell you that because it was in the paper."

Olga decided to make one more attempt to suborn her unwanted visitor.

"What about a little drink, before we start, Algy? Here in my office, not in the restaurant. Armenian cognac is nice. Or vodka. There's quite a selection in my secret cupboard." She rose quickly and grabbed a couple of bottles from the ornate box affixed to the wall.

"Oh, goodness me, no!" said Mr Alberthwaite. "Not at this hour ... er ... er, Olga. And I'm on duty, too. Although I AM a little thirsty. Perhaps a quick glass of orange squash. Just before we get going..."

"I've got just the thing," said Olga, clinking the glasses invitingly. "It's called the Gorbachev vodka-less cordial, it tastes exactly like our ordinary 97% proof vodka, and it makes you feel nice, but it hasn't got alcohol in it, or hardly any. Only one percent."

"How curious! Well, perhaps a little of that, please."

"Just try it," said Olga, doing something dextrous with a vodka bottle while her back was turned towards her guest. "Nice, isn't it?" She settled back on the sofa. "Now tell me, Algy, have you ever been to Russia?"

"No. I've been to Ostend, though. It was a special reduced deal. A weekend with the missus and kids. The sands were lovely. But not as nice as Porthcawl."

"And you went swimming, I suppose."

"We all did."

"I'm sure you've got a strong body, Algy. With lots of muscles... in the right places. Russian women like that."

"This cordial tastes very alcoholic," said Mr. Alberthwaite suspiciously, though he pulled in a little of his midriff flab as well. "Are you sure it's only one per cent?"

"Silly boy! Of course! When you come to Russia, I will give you lots of other good things my grandmother brews in our village. I will be waiting for you at the airport, later we will fly down to the wonderful Black Sea together, and bathe in the warm water. How would you like that?"

"Very nice, I'm sure," said the inspector, politely. (Certainly not one per cent, he thought. Perhaps I shouldn't drink any more? He set it aside for a moment.) "Why is it called the Black Sea, anyway? Is the water really black? I don't think Enid would like it. She doesn't like strange places."

"She wouldn't be coming though, would she?" said Olga helpfully. "You'll see the colour of the water when you get there. Now drink up! Then we can go into the kitchen..."

"My God!" thought Mr. Alberthwaite as he rose to his feet. "I think she's made me drunk. A bit, anyway. I mustn't show it."

Meanwhile, in the kitchen, another small drama was developing.

Chapter Two   **49**

"Here's the kitchen, Mr. Whopp," said Trevor, showing him in. "We need to do a bit of decorating, but it's all kept clean. These nice ladies, Auntie Masha and Auntie Dasha, do the cooking. Both Russian."

The two nice ladies at first looked at the newcomer suspiciously, but then wiped their hands on greasy rags, and came forward to greet him. As twins, they often did things together.

"How do you do, I'm Fred Whopp from the Department of Environmental Health," said the newcomer, and turning to Trevor, he continued, "They're an interesting old couple, aren't they? They look so Russian. Do they speak English?" Trevor had the impression that the deputy inspector wanted to be friendly. If so, it might help the cause.

"Of course, you do, don't you, girls?"

"What?" said Dasha.

"I said, you both speak English," Trevor repeated in a loud voice. "You learned it in Russia, didn't you?"

"We both graduated from the Beef Stroganoff Cookery School in Verkhoyansk," said Masha. "You had to learn it. All the words for food."

"What?" said Dasha, more insistently.

"Shut up, you old fool," Masha whispered in Russian. "He's asking if we speak English. You're supposed to, aren't you! We don't have any language problems with the cooking, Mr. er..."

"Whopp."

"Mr. Whopp." Both women gave a friendly little smile, and looked at him more closely.

50   *Mother Russia*

"Give Mr. Whopp a nice cup of tea," said Trevor. "Sugar and milk, Mr. Whopp?"

"Oh, call me Fred," said Mr. Whopp, smiling cheerfully again. "Milk and two sugars would be fine. Then I'd like to have a quiet look around the kitchen by myself, if you don't mind... er, Trevor. And perhaps make a few helpful suggestions. We're all human, you can't know everything! I imagine Algernon will be tied up for a few minutes."

"Everything very clean and hygienic here, Mr. Whopp," said Masha. "Not like in Russia during the famine. People would eat anything, no matter where they found it. In our village there was an old nun who came around looking for scraps, and one day, when there was no meat, she grabbed a two-month old baby and..."

"You told us that story already," Trevor whispered. "Shut up! We're very careful about the food here," he told the visitor.

Mr. Whopp was looking into the bread cupboard, slightly malodorous on account of old crusts and a green mould at the back.

"This doesn't smell very clean, does it?" he said. "Black bread I imagine. I've never seen it before. It's old and soggy." He sniffed at it. "It smells terrible, doesn't it?"

"Oh," Masha exclaimed, dramatically bursting into tears. "That ever I should have lived to see this day."

"Oh, there, there, Masha," said her sister, with a slightly exaggerated display of concern. "He didn't mean it, I'm sure."

"Oh, you've done it now," Trevor told the deputy inspector. "You've insulted their bread. You mustn't say anything negative about bread to Russians. They can't bear it."

Chapter Two **51**

"Wipe your eyes, dear," said Dasha, proffering her sister the same greasy rag. "Blow your nose in this..." – which she did. "The bread is lovely, it's just that Mr. Whopp never saw black bread before."

"Oh, I'm sorry," said Fred, quite unaware that the little charade had been put on for his benefit. "I didn't mean to offend. It just doesn't smell very fresh, that's all."

"You're only a foreigner," said Masha, with feigned anger. "You can't understand what black bread means to the Russian soul. But how would you like it if someone insulted your bread?"

"We get ours from Tesco's," said Fred. "It's sliced in a packet. You can say what you like about it, no one cares... Now let's see..." He looked around. "Blimey! Is that a saucer of milk on the floor over there? You don't keep a cat on the premises, do you? That's strictly forbidden. I think Mr. Alberthwaite will have to fine you for that. That is..." – he cast a meaningful look at Trevor – "if he finds out."

"Oh no, sir, we haven't got a cat no more," said Masha. "As a matter of fact, it died some time ago, but we forgot to wash its plate. It had a nasty accident. It got hit by a piece of falling metal."

"As long as you haven't got any animals now, there's no problem," said Mr. Whopp. "We won't tell Mr. Alberthwaite, will we? Strictly no animals in food areas. Apart from humans! Ha... ha!" Fred Whopp greatly admired Mr. Alberthwaite's brand of council humour, and sometimes tried to emulate it. "I presume you disposed of the beast carefully. It didn't go into the soup did it? Ha, ha ..." Masha started to wail again. "No, no! Don't get upset! That was just a joke."

"Would you like to try our special rabbit borsch, Urals style," said Auntie Dasha. "You can judge it for yourself."

Mother Russia

She lifted the lid of one of the great pots for him to savour it.

"It does smell nice," said Mr. Whopp, hesitantly. "But I'll refrain, if you don't mind. I mean, all those people were ill after eating it, weren't they? And I'm on duty. Ah, I see you have an icon up on the wall. A little unusual in a restaurant kitchen, but within the regulations, I suppose, if kept clean. Why did you put it there?"

"The Russians consider a holy icon improves the taste of the food," said Trevor quickly, "because God is in it." He went up to look at it more closely and Fred Whopp joined him.

"I think," said Mr. Whopp, after a moment's examination, "it's got bits of fur stuck to the chin. Where did they come from? The rabbits? That could be very bad, Trevor. Bits of rabbits' fur everywhere. Normally we'd issue an immediate enforcement order, you know." He smiled again, rather strangely.

At that moment, Trevor's venture into the restaurant business acquired a new and totally unexpected dimension. Mr. Fred Whopp had been pointing to the scraps of fur, and when he finished speaking he let his arm drop under the normal force of gravity: but when the palm of his hand passed Trevor's left buttock, it paused for a second or two, exerting light but friendly pressure on the flesh. Trevor, being a normal male, comprehended the gesture immediately: though not 'gay' himself, there was no doubting the significance of that little squeeze. In fact there were some pubs in Swansea which were known for it. The young council official was in fact looking for an *amitié particulière* to enliven the inspection.

"Oh God!" thought Trevor. "As if we didn't have enough going on already. And the fate of Mother Russia is in his hands! He and Alberthwaite could dish us – just like

Chapter Two **53**

that! Perhaps I should humour him. He looks harmless enough, anyway."

So rather than pushing the deputy inspector away, or thumping him one (a thought which also crossed his mind), Trevor turned towards him, and said, with an understanding grin.

"Do you have any other hobbies?"

Mr. Whopp, sensing a benign reaction, took the enquiry at its face value.

"Flower arranging and Thai kick-boxing," he said. "And I'm in a gay theatrical group."

He lowered his voice so that the aunties could not hear.

"We're working on a private performance of *Hamlet*. Rosencrantz and Guildenstern will be acting in the nude, except for their florid hats and sword-belts, of course. And Sinclair-Davies, our drag queen, will be playing Ophelia. Would you like a ticket?"

Before the conversation could proceed further, however, Masha was offering her own explanation of the fur on the icon.

"That icon is the Bearded Virgin of Tobolsk," she said. "It's a very popular icon in Russia. She was the only nun ever to grow a beard, so they made her a saint. Some of the beard got lost when we brought it from Russia. But it's pretty, isn't it?"

"Well, get it off the wall before my colleague sees it," Mr. Whopp whispered tensely. "He'll go spare."

In fact Masha just managed to do so before the kitchen door opened, and Olga entered, followed by a slightly wobbly inspector of environmental health. His trilby had moved back over his head to a somewhat rakish angle.

"This way, Algy," said Olga, steadying him by the elbow. "This is our lovely hygienic kitchen. How's the inspection going, Mr. Whopp? Auntie Dasha, Auntie Masha, this is Mr. Alberthwaite, who is also from the council. These are my two aunties from Russia, they do the cooking."

"Nice to meet you," said Mr. Alberthwaite in a slightly thick voice. "Ah-hem... I imagine Mr. Whopp explained that this is a special check-up because we've had a grave complaint about food poisoning. How are things going, Whopp?"

"I'm only just starting, Mr. Alberthwaite. I haven't come across any serious breaches of regulations yet." He looked at Trevor, to be sure that his message was understood.

"So there's nothing to worry about, is there, Mr. Whopp?" said Olga. "We keep everything as clean as birch bark here. Have my aunties been taking care of you? Just like our mother taught us in Russia, so many years ago! Would you like another glass of cordial, Algy? I've brought the bottle."

"I think we should get on with the inspection," said Mr. Alberthwaite, his voice as slurred as ever.

Life in Salubrious Passage, however, as the reader has no doubt already observed, had a propensity to change direction rapidly, and at this point in our tale it happened again. Events in the kitchen were disrupted by a loud banging on the door which led into the dining room. Shrieks of alarm could be heard among the Russians seated there.

"Help!" cried an agitated voice. "Is anyone there? Come quick!"

Everybody rushed out of the kitchen to find the luncheon celebrations in considerable disarray. Or, to state facts more accurately, a fight was going on between the two patriarchal figures: Viktor Viktorovich, red as a beetroot, and, grasping a lavatory pan, he was struggling with Genadii Genadievich, who was trying to prise the ceramic object from him. The ladies were endeavouring to separate them, while the priest and the poet made unheeded appeals for Christian charity and calm. The little girls were white-faced and sobbing with fear.

"Let go, you fool!" Genadii Genadievich was saying. "You'll never get away with it. Give it to me! Think of your heart! You'll be ill! You can't steal a big thing like that, you'll be noticed!"

"Well, it's mine," gasped Viktor Viktorovich. "If you hadn't made such a fuss, I could have got it into the car without anyone noticing!"

"What the hell is going on here?" asked Trevor.

"He was only trying to steal the lavatory pan," Olga panted, as she joined the fray. "He's drunk, you see. He can't help it, he's got a bathroom fittings fixation. He was a plumber in the bad old days, when Stalin was in power, and you couldn't get a decent pan for love nor money. There were thieves who specialised in them. I had friends who were pan-burgled, and the thieves didn't take anything else. Wait a minute, Trevor darling, we'll get it sorted out. Viktor Viktorovich," she shrieked. "Stop it, straight away!"

"Sanitary fittings!" said Mr. Alberthwaite, astonished. "And stealing them from catering premises! Did he cap the soil pipe properly? It's against regulations. Are there other adequate washing facilities? We'll have to inspect them immediately. We can issue an enforcement order. I

56   *Mother Russia*

don't know, though..." he added weakly. "I'm not feeling too well. I think it was the cordial."

In fact his knees sagged and he sank slowly to the floor. "Whopp. Whopp, give me a hand, will you? It's me knees!"

"I'm sure there'll be no need for an enforcement order, Mr. Alberthwaite," said Mr. Whopp, as he tried without success to help his superior get back onto his feet. "I'm sure the management can get it capped in an hour or two, with one of the emergency services."

Trevor had the impression that the remark was addressed to him.

By now, Viktor Viktorovich was on the floor himself, desperately hugging the pan and turning a little blue with effort. Suddenly he released it, his head fell back, and he lay motionless.

"Oh, my God!" exclaimed one of the Russian women. "He's had another heart attack! Viktor Viktorovich, wake up!" Someone started slapping his cheek. "Can we try artificial respiration? Get an ambulance, someone!"

Trevor glanced at the two bodies on the floor, Viktor Viktorovich's and Algernon Alberthwaite's, and dashed to the telephone to order an ambulance for two. "Jesus," he thought, "if that's a Russian lunch party, we don't want any more!"

The vehicle arrived, siren blaring, a few minutes later, just as Viktor Viktorovich was coming to. The ambulance men rushed in, and, assessing the situation, – one heart attack and one drunk – produced two stretchers.

"What nice, clean stretchers," said Olga. "When Viktor Viktorovich knows what's happened to him, he'll be delighted having his heart attack here. I mean, he wouldn't get emergency treatment like that in Russia. You

Chapter Two **57**

are going with him to the hospital, are you, Genadii Genadievich?"

The ambulance men, after a brief check for breathing, got Viktor Viktorovich onto the stretcher and carried him out, followed by his elderly companion. Then they came back for the second case.

"Algy is all right, I think," said Olga. "He's just drunk. He can get onto the stretcher himself, if you lay it on the floor. Come on Algy, roll yourself over! I think you'll only have to take him back to the Civic Centre."

"No, it'll have to be the hospital," said one of the ambulance men. "He'll have to see a doctor."

"Who?" said Mr. Alberthwaite, in a daze. "Where's my briefcase? Enid put me lunch in it. Here it is! Whopp, you stay here and complete the inspection."

When the two had been taken off, Viktor Viktorovich to enjoy the cardiac arrest facilities at the local hospital, and Mr. Alberthwaite to sober up in the emergency waiting room, the Russian guests settled down again and finished their lunch. Olga made up the bill, the guests collected their things and trooped off, rather subdued. Everybody had looked forward to an exciting lunch, but not excitement of that order.

When they had gone, the restaurant again seemed strangely quiet, apart from the clink of dishes in the kitchen. A sort of normality was returning. Olga, Trevor, Mr. Whopp looked at one another.

"Well, we'll have to get someone to put the pan back," said Trevor finally, looking at the forlorn object lying on the floor.

"Oh, get it done as soon as you reasonably can," said Mr. Whopp, in a comforting tone. "The restaurant is closed at the moment, anyway. Really, we should be issuing a closure order, but what with Mr. Alberthwaite's indisposition, and the emergency heart case, I think we'll book you in for another inspection in a few days' time. By then," he added in a stage whisper, "you'll have things cleaned up a bit, won't you? We in the council like to have..." – he paused fractionally – "...good relations with the ratepayers. The better, the better, if you see what I mean."

There was a moment's silence as Olga – and more particularly Trevor – considered the implication of his words.

"I think I'll be off, then," said Mr. Whopp. "I haven't had my lunch break yet. I suppose I should go back to the office. I'll put in an interim report, without any recommendations. They will come later."

"Perhaps a little rabbit soup before you go?" Olga suggested.

"Oh no," said Mr. Whopp hurriedly. "I'll have a snack in our cafeteria. Well, 'bye then." He flashed another smile in Trevor's direction. "I'll contact you next week."

And the door closed behind him.

Trevor and Olga sat down at one of the tables for a moment's relaxation.

"We don't want many more parties like that," said Trevor.

"Why not," said Olga, brightly. "They paid their bill, didn't they? We did quite well out of it."

"By the way, Olga," Trevor remarked. "That Russian hasn't come back to pick up his briefcase, has he?"

Chapter Two **59**

The question was strangely apposite: at that very moment they heard a vehicle pull up outside. Trevor glanced through the window. A battered white van had stopped outside with "Penclawdd Cockle and Laverbread Company" painted on it. There was a crude drawing of an out-size cockle (admittedly a creature not easily depicted) on the bonnet. At first, no one got out: evidently, some sort of discussion was going on in the cab. Then there was a faint roar of laughter, suggesting a joke.

"Cockles and laverbread!" said Olga, looking over Trevor's shoulder. "It must be Ivan Kravchenko."

At that moment the door of the van opened and three men emerged. It was indeed Ivan Ivanovich, accompanied by two henchmen, both younger than he, in their thirties, and clad in sweaters with a cockle emblem on them. They had some physical resemblance – blue eyes, fair hair, and heavy faces and they may have been related - brothers, perhaps. "A tough pair," thought Trevor, "such as you might expect to find in the coarser reaches of the boxing world."

"He's come back to fetch his briefcase," Olga continued. "I don't know the others, though." Trevor could see she was uneasy again.

"But all we have to do is give him his briefcase and cutting tools," said Trevor. "And that should be the end of that!"

"I wonder," said Olga. "There's his business proposition as well."

The bell rang, and Olga herself opened the door. Ivan Ivanovich was the first to enter, his heavy jowls wreathed in a smile.

"Oh, hullo, Ivan Ivanich," she said, graciously. "I'm so sorry about the soup, yesterday. Very ill-behaved

60   *Mother Russia*

children, not like the ones in Russia. We've had some delightful little Russian girls in to lunch today, haven't we, Trevor? Has your suit gone to the cleaners? We'll pay, of course."

"Oh, that suit has had more on it than soup," said Ivan Ivanich, with a strange laugh. "Don't worry, Olga Vasilievna, it wiped off all right when I got home. No offence taken, you know what we are like in Russia."

Olga looked questioningly at his unprepossessing companions.

"These boys work for me, this is Llew," he said, pointing to the large one, "and this is Morgan. I met them in Neath. They were both out of work, so I've given them jobs in the company."

The new employees nodded in agreement.

"What company is that?" asked Olga.

"Penclawdd Cockles," said Ivan. "I told you about it." His companions sniggered.

"What *are* cockles, exactly?" said Olga, turning to Trevor. "Are they like oysters?"

"You could say that," said Trevor, "but smaller, and they don't cost so much. When my mother was alive we used to have them for breakfast on a Saturday. You fry them up with bread crumbs."

"Very nice, too," said Ivan. "I've got to like them myself. I never saw anything like them in Russia." He puffed out his chest a little. "We'll export them to Moscow and the provinces. It will be a great novelty".

"Extraordinary," said Trevor. "Cockles to Russia! I would never have believed it."

Chapter Two **61**

Llew and Morgan were looking around the restaurant – it was clear that they had never been in Russian surroundings before.

"Strange, isn't it?" said Llew.

"Is that a real bear skin?" asked Morgan.

"Of course," said Olga. "It came from Siberia."

"Jesus!" said Llew. "Dangerous things them bears, mind! Look at the fangs. And the claws. That skin must be worth a bob or two, though. I never seen one before."

"Have you got anything for us to drink," asked Morgan, suddenly.

Trevor picked up a menu, and would have handed it to him, but the new-found director of the cockle business waved it off dismissively.

"Oh no, Trevor," said Olga, quickly. "No menu, it's on the house! Ivan Ivanovich and his friends are our guests. What shall it be, a glass of whiskey, vodka? A gin and tonic?"

"I think a few cans of lager this time of day," said Ivan. "Okay boys?"

He covered his mouth with his hand and whispered to Olga: "If they start on spirits now, they may get a bit out of hand."

"Three lagers from the fridge, auntie," Olga shouted into the kitchen. She needn't have raised her voice, however, because Dasha and Masha were assessing the younger men from behind the half-open kitchen door. "Just a minute," said Dasha. "We'll bring it!"

"I think I left my briefcase here last night," said Ivan. "Under the table. Did you find it?"

62   *Mother Russia*

"Of course, Ivan Ivanovich! We've kept it for you safe and sound."

"You didn't go nosing around in it, I hope," said Ivan. "I didn't lock it. There's some confidential documents in there."

"We never look in people's lost property," Olga said coldly, "unless there's a special need. And we knew this was yours. When customers leave things here they are set aside to be picked up later. In fact, we have quite a collection – three umbrellas, a parrot cage, and two gross Durex in a large packet. I'll go and get the briefcase," she added. "It's in the office."

"I'll come with you", said Ivan. "I want to talk to you about our cockles again."

"Oh!" said Olga, her heart sinking. "Then Trevor must come too, he's a partner now."

When all three had retired to the little room under the stairs and closed the door, Ivan assumed a conspiratorial air.

"Commercial matters have to be treated in confidence," he said. "There's a lot of money involved, and I've got rivals."

It had never occurred to Trevor that there might be a lot of money, or rivalry, in the cockle business, and the secrecy seemed a bit excessive.

"Your company's based in Penclawdd, is it?" he asked.

"Yes. We've taken over some old premises. In fact, it's a disused chapel with a pulpit. It's our staff quarters and warehouse."

"Do you go out picking the cockles yourself?" Trevor asked somewhat incautiously.

Chapter Two **63**

"Certainly not," said Ivan, his face assuming a nasty expression. "I do the business side – the transport, and contact with Russia. We have labour for cockle-picking."

"You distribute locally as well?" said Trevor.

"A lot around Swansea and Neath," said Ivan. "The rest of the stuff will be going off to Russia. I'll be doing a monthly cockle run to Moscow, through Belgium, Germany and Poland. The van is refrigerated, so that the stuff don't go off. Some of the Welsh cockles will go all the way through to Verkhoyansk in the Urals. What do you think of that?"

Trevor looked at Olga with obvious disbelief.

"Oh, Ivan Ivanich is a great businessman," said Olga, supportively. "What a venture!"

"Do you bring anything back?" asked Trevor.

"Of course," said Ivan. "You can't leave a rich country like Russia empty-handed, can you? Tins of caviar and smoked sturgeon. That's what you'll be getting to sell here."

"Will we?" said Trevor.

There was a little silence. The *izba* clock ticked in the corner, and suddenly the icon lamp seemed to cast a red, rather devilish glow on Ivan Ivanich's face.

"Any problems with the customs?" asked Trevor, momentarily at a loss.

"Customs?" said Ivan Ivanich. "Who said anything about customs? I've got my own channels... both ways."

"I think it's a wonderful idea, Ivan Ivanovich," said Olga. "But I really don't think we'll be able to sell any Russian seafood. Our customers wouldn't be rich enough."

64   *Mother Russia*

Ivan Ivanovich took no notice of her whatever.

"Of course," he said, "if you'll be keeping expensive stuff like that on the premises, you'll need protection."

"Protection?!" said Trevor. Ivan Ivanovich's bombshell – for it was no less – was followed by a longer silence.

"Things are a bit difficult, like I said," Ivan continued. "We're getting competition from those Ukrainians in Neath."

"Ukrainians in Neath?" Trevor repeated.

"They live in a bed and breakfast by the station," Ivan explained. "And a pretty nasty lot they are. Knife fights and all that sort of thing. It's been in the papers. They'd be down here like a shot if they found you had caviar and sturgeon – that is, if you were not protected. Mother Russia is an obvious place for them to come, isn't it?"

Olga and Trevor exchanged glances.

"If there's anything we won't need, it's protection," said Trevor. "Caviar and sturgeon? We won't be able to sell it anyway, Olga told you. The local people aren't used to it, and it's too dear for them. We have a problem even with the borsch."

"Well, you must try," said Ivan imperiously. "Like the other places I've got. And the boys have set their hearts on protecting you. It's best not to annoy them."

He looked around expressively and the "boys" nodded. "They won't be here all the time. You only have to give them a few drinks and feed them when they ask. We'll see how things go."

He rose from his seat and looked at his watch, indicating, as it were, that the business discussion was over. "We'll call in tomorrow with the first batch. Boys," he called out as all three left the office, "ready, are you?"

Chapter Two **65**

A few minutes later the three of them had gone, leaving the proprietors of Mother Russia with yet another worry on their minds.

Chapter Three

(Mainly concerning a large fridge, fortune-telling, and a fire)

Swansea has thriving colonies of sea-gulls, which daily wing their way over the open waters of the bay, across the grey-green expanse of Kilvey Hill, and indeed over the roofs of Salubrious Passage. Had any of them swooped down to the office window of Mother Russia and perched on the sill, the day after the party, they would have detected a lively row going on between the humans inside.

"Oh, Trevor, you must try!" (That would have been Olga's voice, appealing.) "Mr Whopp is quite nice, and Shakespeare is the national poet."

"Yes, yes!" cried two elderly female voices of the aunts. "For the good of Mother Russia."

"*Not bloody likely!*" shouted a man (Trevor.) "I don't want Fred Whopp and I'm not that way inclined."

It was clearly three against one.

"We had to put up with worse than that in the Revolution," said Masha. "A Red Army Colonel fell in love with my brother, and our family was of aristocratic background. But since the communists were winning, and we needed the ration cards, my brother had to go through with it. I'm glad to say they lived together happily for years. And my brother's girl-friend never held it against him. He married her later when he straightened himself out."

"In fact," said Dasha, "we all wanted them to go on meeting, because the colonel got us better rations."

68   *Mother Russia*

"Well, I have no intention of living happily ever after with Fred Whopp," said Trevor, icily. "Even to save Mother Russia."

The atmosphere in the little office was tense indeed, and the battle unequal. The point was that Dasha had glimpsed Mr. Whopp's brief grope, and had hastened to tell Olga about it. Everyone understood its implications – that is, in terms of licences and residence permits. Fred Whopp's support could be vital, and they were now telling Trevor his bounden duty.

"Trevushka, he's obviously taken a liking to you," said Olga, persuasively. "If he really falls in love with you, you'll be able to ask him to get a licence for the restaurant. Support from the council could help us get residence permits, too."

"I don't know about Russia," said Trevor, "but things aren't as easy as that in Swansea. You can't pressure officials. It's illegal."

"There's nothing illegal about love," said Dasha, "between men or women, too. I think he's a very nice young man. In fact, quite lovable."

"Who said anything about love, for God's sake?!" said Trevor. "I hardly know him. And I'm not queer. Or 'gay' as they say."

"Don't put it like that, darling," said Olga, "and get yourself all worked up. Of course we all know you're not... queer, not at all. So all you have to do is be a bit friendly, let him sit close to you and squeeze your hand, and things like that."

"Oh yes?" said Trevor, defiantly.

"Well, just for a bit," said Olga. "And see what happens."

Chapter Three **69**

"I've never been groped by a fella, ever," said Trevor.

"Well you were today," said Olga.

They all fell silent, and Trevor looked at the three faces in front of him: six blue Slav eyes gazed at him intently, in hope. These women depend on me, after all, he thought. And in his heart of hearts he knew that he couldn't let them down.

"All right," he said slowly. "I'll give Fred Whopp a ring, and suggest we meet for a drink. But in one of the ordinary pubs, no funny business. And I'm certainly not going to see that 'Hamlet in drag' thing."

"What's 'drag'" said Olga.

"Men dressed as women."

"It might be quite artistic," said Olga. "I wouldn't mind seeing it myself."

"I wouldn't mind seeing it, either," said Masha, while her sister nodded vigorously in agreement.

"I dare say you wouldn't, all of you," said Trevor, "but you can't. It's by invitation only. And I don't suppose there will be a single woman in the audience. It would be too embarrassing for them. But as I say, I'll see Fred Whopp, just to help things along."

There was an obvious sense of relief among the ladies.

"Oh, Trevor, you are wonderful!" said Olga. "You are our saviour." She grabbed him by the neck, (they were sitting on the sofa again), and pulled him towards her.

"I haven't saved anything yet..," he gasped. The two aunts leaned over the sofa and hugged him from behind, making the pressures on him almost unbearable. Trevor thought the seat would collapse, but managed to extricate himself before it did so.

70 *Mother Russia*

"We've still got to solve the problem of takings while the restaurant is closed," he said. "How much have we taken this week so far? "

"About a hundred and twenty pounds, including the celebration lunch," Olga replied.

"Jesus, is that all?"

There was silence in the little office as they all thought about it.

"I'm sure this Russian fish thing is not going to help," Trevor added. "It's hopeless even when we re-open. Caviar and sturgeon will be far too dear, and who's going to come to a Russian restaurant for cockles and laverbread?"

"We shouldn't have agreed to take it, Olga. When Ivan and his mates come next time we tell them to go away."

"Impossible, Trevor! Impossible," cried Olga. "Especially with the protection. You can't tell people like them to go away. Remember what we found in the brief case."

"He wouldn't dare..," Trevor began.

"Oh yes he would," said Olga. I've seen a lot like him in Russia. They're ruthless."

There was a moment's silence.

"Perhaps some live musical entertainment," said Trevor. "Not just the tapes... Can anyone play anything?"

"We had a piano in the family when I was a girl, but my father drank it away," said Olga. "So I never learned."

"I used to play the banjo," said Trevor uncertainly, "but that's out of fashion now. What about our aunties?" he looked at Masha and Dasha.

"The balalaika a bit," said Masha. "But not well enough for a superior restaurant like ours."

"Auntie Dasha, you used to tell fortunes," said Olga. "You used to go to the great fair at Nizhnii Novgorod, didn't you?"

"Fortune-telling," said Trevor, his face lighting up. "Yes, you've got an idea there! I'm sure there's no genuine fortune-teller in Swansea. A Russian fortune teller. In a sort of gypsy costume. It might go like a bomb. There's been a great spiritual vacuum since most of the chapels closed, especially among the more nervy types. Just the kind who like to have their fortunes told. A fortune-telling booth could tide us over. I'm sure we wouldn't need a licence for it."

"But even if we did," said Olga, triumphantly, "Mr. Whopp could help us, couldn't he?"

It was fortunate that the discussion should have reached a conclusion just then, because the attention of the participants was distracted by the sound, now familiar, of a van stopping outside. Olga went to the window.

"Oh, it's Ivan Kravchenko," she said. "They must have brought the sturgeon and the caviar! I didn't think they'd be back so soon!"

She and Trevor went out into the Passage.

Llew and Morgan, in their white jerseys as before, were unlocking the back door of the vehicle, a little unsteadily, it seemed, as though they had been drinking, which was probably the case.

"Hello," Olga greeted them. "You've brought the caviar and the sturgeon, have you?"

They did not answer, but climbed inside the freight compartment. Trevor looked on with interest: pots of

72   *Mother Russia*

caviar were rarely on view in Swansea, and he had never actually seen a sturgeon. He somehow expected one of the men to reappear with huge, shark-like creature on his shoulders. Instead, there was a sound of a heavy object, possibly a box, being shifted.

"It's not just the sturgeon and caviar, love," said Morgan, sticking his head out. "We've brought you a nice fridge to keep it in. Llew, get the trolley out, will you?"

He jumped down. "Okay. He said can we have a look at the kitchen, to see where it can go?"

"A fridge?" asked Olga, looking helplessly at Trevor. "Ivan Ivanovich didn't say anything about a fridge!"

"How old is it?" said Trevor.

He and Olga looked into the back of the van, where another unpleasant surprise awaited them: the fridge was not one of those small neat appliances which could be stuck in a corner, but a large appliance of many cubic feet.

"We can't have that," said Trevor. "There's no room for it. You don't need a big fridge like that for caviar, anyway. We'll have to tell Ivan. Where is he?"

"Oh, he'll be here in a minute," said Llew. "He's following us in his new car."

And sure enough, a moment later, a sleek Mercedes edged its way into the Passage. The owner got out nonchalantly; he was clad in another smart suit, and showed his usual commanding smile.

"Here we are," he said. "Everything arrived safe and sound. Olga, can we have a look at the kitchen, to see where it can go?"

"You never said anything about a fridge," said Trevor, angrily. "Especially one of that size."

Chapter Three **73**

"Oh, it's better to keep the caviar separate from everything else, on its own. It has to be kept at a special temperature. Expensive stuff. And the sturgeon. There may be quite a lot of it. Okay, boys, get it out now. Mind you don't dent it! It cost me a packet!"

"Well, we won't have it," said Trevor. "It'll have to go back."

Ivan's benign demeanour vanished immediately, as it had done during the borsch episode. He beckoned to the two helpers and in an instant the three of them had grabbed Trevor and pushed him roughly against the wall. He struggled to free himself, but in vain. There was nothing Olga could do except look on, terrified. Llew and Morgan held him there, while Ivan thrust his face close, grinning unpleasantly. Then, without saying a word, he slipped his hand into his breast pocket and withdrew it a little, so that Trevor could just glimpse the white bone sheath of a razor.

"Want some of this, do you?" Ivan asked.

Trevor had never been so frightened in his life, though he tried not to show it. He looked over Ivan's shoulder: Salubrious Passage was deserted, and there was no one else in sight. The Mercedes and the van provided some element of concealment from Wind Street, anyway. Only the gulls overhead could witness what was happening. Trevor heard Olga's tremulous voice. "Let them take it in, Trevor. We'll find place for it somehow."

Trevor looked again at the hard faces confronting him: if he did not yield, he could easily be beaten up, possibly disfigured.

"Typical," thought Trevor. "Not a copper in sight."

"All right," he said aloud. "I agree."

74   *Mother Russia*

In a flash the atmosphere had changed again, and Ivan was affability itself. Olga relaxed visibly.

"There, what's your name, Trevor? No problem, see." He beckoned to Llew and Morgan to step back and release him. "Okay, boys, get it in, careful now, it's quite heavy." The two hefties got the unwieldy object onto the trolley and trundled it carefully through the restaurant and into the kitchen. The others followed.

In the kitchen itself Ivan and his helpers faced more opposition. The aunties, whom they had just glimpsed on their first visit to the premises, were glad to see them – but not the fridge.

"Back again, boys," said Dasha with a questioning look. "What's this?"

"Ivan Ivanovich is giving us a fridge to keep the caviar and sturgeon in," Olga explained.

Masha looked at it disapprovingly. "We can't have this. It's enormous. There's nowhere to put it."

"You don't need a great big fridge to keep caviar, boys," said Dasha. "We'll be bloody lucky if we sell two pots a year. Or the sturgeon. The people around here don't even know what it is."

"Oh, it's all been decided," said Ivan. "Don't interfere."

"Oh no it hasn't," said Masha.

The two henchmen exchanged uncertain glances, and looked at their boss. Should the two old crones be folded and thrown out, while the appliance was being installed, or should they be humoured? Olga came to the rescue.

"Now, aunties," she said. "It has all been decided, really. Ivan Ivanovich says the fridge is needed, and he knows best. I think there's just enough room for it in the corner."

Chapter Three **75**

So the installation took place precisely as Ivan ordered. When the fridge had been edged into a corner and plugged in, the little group – Olga, Trevor, the aunts, and the three men – stood back and looked at it.

"Well, it looks professional," said Trevor grudgingly. "But what's that? A padlock?" Indeed, the fridge had been fitted with a hasp from which hung a strong brass padlock. "Why does it have to be locked?"

"To prevent theft, of course," said Ivan. "You get all sorts of dishonest people around these days. As a matter of fact, I'll be keeping it locked most of the time."

"Will we have a key, too?" asked Olga.

"No."

"But how can we get at the caviar and the sturgeon if it's locked up?" said Trevor.

"Well, you won't be selling much of it, will you," said Ivan. "You said so yourself. We'll give you a bit to keep in your own fridge, if anyone asks. It hasn't come in from Russia yet."

"But if the fridge is empty," asked Olga, "why is it so heavy?"

"And if we're keeping some of the stuff in our own fridge, we won't need yours!" said Trevor. "Especially if we can't get into it. You said it had to be kept at a special temperature."

Ivan's mood changed again, and going up to Trevor, he ran his fingers over Trevor's Ukrainian neckband. "I wouldn't worry too much about the technical details, if I was you," he growled. "Don't ask so many questions. Too much worry killed the cat, didn't it?" And with that he gave Trevor a little push backwards, playful, yet

76 *Mother Russia*

threatening. Llew and Morgan looked on in some amusement.

"It's best not to annoy Ivan," said Llew. "He's a bit quick-tempered, like."

"Yes," added Morgan, "quick-tempered."

Trevor was boiling, but there was nothing he could do. Olga was again almost in tears.

"Olga," said Ivan, "give the boys a few bottles of beer to drink in the van, will you? It's thirsty work, moving fridges. I don't think they'll have anything to eat today. Then we'll be off. We've got a lot of cockles to sell this afternoon."

The two helpers laughed, and they all went back into the dining room.

Much to Trevor's relief, the three men took their bottles and made their way towards the door, without sitting down. "See you again soon, boys!" Masha called out. As they left, Ivan turned back.

"Olga," he said. "I nearly forgot. Do you have a spare key to the premises?"

"What for?" asked Trevor quickly. "No, we haven't."

"We may have to get to the fridge at awkward hours, when no one is here," said Ivan. "A load might come in from Russia late, see. We wouldn't like to get you out of bed. Come on, let's have a key."

"Here you are, Ivan Ivanovich," said Olga fumbling in a handbag.

He took it from her, pocketed it, and the three of them finally left. Trevor and Olga watched them go.

"So what happens now?" said Trevor. "We're landed with his fridge as well. God knows what's in it."

Chapter Three **77**

"I've got no idea," said Olga. "We can only hope for the best. I think we had better get down to the market and get some food in. Me, you, and Masha. Dasha will get busy."

"And what will she be doing?" said Trevor.

"Her first fortune-telling appointment is at three," Olga replied. "I think she's best left alone for that. The client might not wish to be overheard."

Birds are sharp-eyed creatures, but they are naturally bereft of reading skills. Had the sea-gulls which perched on roofs near Salubrious Passage been able to peruse text, however, they would have noted, that very afternoon, a significant addition to the Mother Russia façade. A new sign appeared above the doorway. It read:

FORTUNE-TELLER

by

Auntie Dasha from the Volga

Crystal gazing, palms, and dreams interpreted.

Contact with the dead relatives.

Moderate rates.

By appointment only, see telephone number below.

And inside the restaurant, had the birds been able to flutter in, they would have found, in one corner, a little booth with a heavy plush curtain designed to exclude curious gazes. Soon after the others had gone off to the

78 *Mother Russia*

market, Dasha emerged from the office, which (as the reader will by now know) also served as a changing room. She was colourfully beshawled, with a floral kerchief over her head, and blackened areas around her eyes to make them look more mysterious. A little unsteadily, because she had just downed a couple of rums, she went over to the booth and cast a final glance inside it. There were two rustic stools, a little round table, and a large crystal ball, miraculously procured from one of Swansea's remaining pawnbrokers. A couple of candles and an artificial pineapple completed the intimate decor. "Exotic fruit," she had told Olga, "was part of the hallowed tradition of fortune-telling." A mirror reflected the candle and other-worldly decor, adding an eerie dimension of its own. A little stack of packets and phials completed the picture.

"Nice and mysterious," thought Dasha. "Just what customers would expect. Pity there haven't been any, except this woman who's coming shortly. I think I'll start the rissoles while I have time. They can simmer while I'm doing the reading."

She went into the deserted kitchen, took a generous portion of sausage meat from the Mother Russia fridge, and by chance glanced up at a shelf above the stove. A bottle label caught her eye, with the cheerful likeness of an eighteenth-century pirate on it. "Captain Morgan's Rum," she read. Perhaps as a result of her pre-prandial tipple, she had the distinct impression that the Captain winked at her. Without further ado, she took the bottle, poured a generous amount into the minced meat, and put it back on the shelf, though somewhat carelessly. Then she rolled the meat into balls and dropped them into a fat-filled frying pan. No sooner had she lit the gas under them than the door-bell rang. "It must be my client," she thought, excitedly. "I wonder what she's like?" She ran out to look.

Chapter Three **79**

On opening the door she found a plump, bespectacled, young woman dressed in a black sweater and bulging jeans. The client's manner was furtive and embarrassed: evidently, she would not want anyone to know about her visit. So Dasha greeted her somewhat peremptorily and led her to the booth, leaving fuller introductions until later.

As Dasha was shortly to learn, her client was Gloria Evans, a cub reporter on the Evening Post, the offices of which were but a few hundred yards from Salubrious Passage. Gloria had decided to make a quick, unobserved visit to the fortune-teller to ascertain, if possible, the prospects for an emotional attachment. Although pushing forty, she had never had a proper boyfriend, but lately she had fallen hopelessly in love with Ivor Jones, an eligible bachelor from the distribution department. Unfortunately, he was only twenty, and looking for someone younger than himself. So whenever his eye passed over Gloria, it scarcely flickered.

In professional terms Gloria was always on the look-out for stories, and she had decided that if the fortune-teller's reading wasn't any good, she could in any case write it up as an anonymous paragraph for the "Swansea Day by Day" page. Given the lack of incidents, the "Day by Day" page was usually desperate for copy.

Dasha swished back the plush curtain, and patted her client gently in. Gloria lowered herself onto one of the little Russian stools, her ample posterior all but concealing it. Then Dasha sat down opposite her, behind the little table, and glanced knowingly into the crystal ball. Gloria, for her part, was quite impressed by the mysterious and diminutive figure opposite: it was exactly what she had hoped for. So far so good...

"Hello, hello," said Dasha with a weird smile, and posed, in a deliberately croaky voice, a shower of

80 *Mother Russia*

questions. "What is your name? Are you troubled by something? Matters of the heart? Do you want to look into the future, or explore the meaning of the past? Dreams, perhaps? Have you ever had your fortune told before? Tell me all, my dear!"

Gloria gave her name, and, without going further into her emotional deserts, she said that she would like to have her palm read so as to know what she might expect from life in the future. She asked whether Miss Dasha had been reading palms for long.

"Yes," said Dasha. "I'm a gypsy from Russia and my family has been telling fortunes for generations. Ivan the Terrible had his fortune told by my great, great, great (she paused, as though to count), great, great grandmother."

"Really!" said Gloria. "I don't suppose many families go back as far as that here. To remember, I mean. I know about Ivan the Terrible – he was sixteenth century."

"First, let me look deep into your eyes and take your zodiac measure," said Dasha, so as to move things forward. "The eyes are the windows to the sould."

Gloria was uncertain about zodiac measures, but guessed that 'sould' was supposed to be 'soul'. Dasha thrust her wizened visage closer.

"What is your name, again?" she repeated.

"Gloria Evans," said Gloria.

"Ah, yes," said Dasha, remembering that she knew it already. "What a sweet sound that makes, Gloria Evans. Nobody in Russia is called Gloria Evans, not a sould, I am sure, from Brest to Vladivostok. A sweet name is a great blessing in life. But I'm sure you have many others."

"Oh, I don't know," said Gloria. "I have many problems, too."

Chapter Three **81**

"Stop," said Dasha, opening her eyes wide and raising her beshawled arms dramatically. "We'll come to those in a minute. When is your birthday? "

"25 July, 1960."

"The year doesn't matter. You're a Leo, a lion, a lioness. Strong-willed, decisive, successful in the hunt."

"I haven't been very successful at the Evening Post," said Gloria.

"I see success for you in the future," said Dasha, peering into the ball. "Lots of interesting news! Big articles to make you famous. But let's look into your past. I see a lovely garden, with flowers and vegetables, a lovely home. I think you've had a happy family life."

"Really?" said Gloria, amazed. "My father was a gardener, he grew prize begonias."

"I know these things," said Dasha, authoritatively, though I've never tasted one." She was delighted to have scored a hit, albeit at random.

"Did anyone in the family have a squint? I see a squinting eye looking at me through the crystal ball."

"No," said Gloria. "No one squinted... though" – she paused excitedly. "Yes, my great aunt Edna did. I can just remember it as a child. It frightened the life out of me."

Dasha felt that although this was only her first client, things were going rather well. She looked at Gloria's podgy fingers and checked for rings: several glinted in the candle-light, but there were none to indicate engagement or marriage. The chances are, she thought, that this girl has come to ask about love and marriage.

"The picture is becoming clearer," said Dasha, after a meaningful pause. "Birds!" (That was another good ploy: they usually fitted in somewhere.)

82   *Mother Russia*

"Birds?" Gloria repeated. "What kind of birds? Chickens, ducks, geese? Christmas poultry? We always had a turkey for Christmas."

"Well," said Dasha, "I see feathered creatures... Beautiful ones! Perhaps, love-birds flying over a river. Or swans."

"That would be the River Urgue that ran through our village," said Gloria. "When I was a girl. But I can't remember any love-birds, or swans. There were some brown ducks."

"No," said Dasha, staring ever more intently into the glass. "It's clearer now. Swan Lake, the ballet by the great Russian composer Tchaikovsky. I see a beautiful ballet dancer in white. Did you ever dance at all?"

"Only the waltz and foxtrot," said Gloria, "at the Trocadero Dance Hall."

"Well," said Dasha, "A handsome young man has come into the picture. You should see him when you next go to the dance hall. He could be, yes, a partner for you in the dance of life."

"Oh, really," said Gloria, almost breathless. "Can you see his face? Is he square jawed, with a big nose, and going a bit thin on top?"

"Thin on top?" said Dasha.

"A bit bald."

"Yes, yes!"

"Oh," said Gloria. "Then I know exactly whom you mean."

Dasha looked at her triumphantly.

"I think we are getting on very well," she said. "And other people about you," she continued, rather

Chapter Three **83**

unexpectedly. "Do you have any brothers or sisters? I still sense a warm family atmosphere." She raised her elbows a little, like a hen sheltering a young brood.

"No," said Gloria, "but I share the house with my two uncles. They're much older."

Dasha gave her another penetrating glance.

"I see handsome men coming out of your front door," she said. Gloria paused for a moment. Ivor had never come out of her front door because he had never been inside the house.

"Well," she said, "that must be Uncle Dave and Uncle Charlie, they're both handsome. In fact, one of them used to work for Burtons Tailors."

"And their wives," said Dasha, penetrating further. "You have kindly aunts as well?"

"Oh no, both my aunties are dead," said Gloria. "My uncles are single again."

Dasha bent low over the table. "I foresee a late union for both of them," she said tersely. "Unusual matches, but happy ones." She leaned back and looked up. "You must bring them along here for lunch one day when we re-open. I'm sure they'd like it."

"They don't like exotic food."

"We may be starting fish and chips soon," said Dasha, and, forgetting herself a little: "I suppose they both have pensions?"

Gloria gave the fortune teller a strange look. "Why the hell is she going on about my uncles?" she thought. "And pensions? I'm the one who's having their bloody fortune told. It's no business of hers."

84 *Mother Russia*

"I'm not sure about that," she said. "They've both got enough to live on. But I'd like to know what is going to happen to ME! Can you tell me anything more about Ivor Evans?"

"Who's Ivor Evans?"

"He's the man I'm hoping to foxtrot with at the Trocadero tonight."

Dasha looked into her crystal ball again, and deep in thought fingered the pineapple.

"You're in love with him, aren't you?" she asked with an air of absolute prescience.

"Yes," Gloria admitted.

"Do you happen to know when his birthday is?"

"It's 19 November. Sometimes we have little birthday celebrations at the office."

"Excellent," said Dasha. "He's a Scorpio... I may be able to help you."

Gloria gazed at her intently.

"Do you get close to him at work?"

"Well, yes." Gloria thought: "As close as I can." And she giggled.

"And do you normally wear scent?"

"I buy Wild Jungle Fragrance at Jim's Discount Store," said Gloria. "But I haven't used it recently. The cat knocked the bottle over, and a lot of it got wasted."

"Well," said Dasha. "Now we know his zodiac sign, I think I can help you. I have some Russian love-potions for young ladies in need. The potions are traditional and the secret has been kept for hundreds of years. The only thing

Chapter Three **85**

is, they have to match the young man's stars. We can do that now."

She turned to the little collection of different coloured phials, and picked out one at random.

"This is the one you need. If you put this on every day, and get close to the gentleman of your choice, you will notice a strong upsurge in his affection for you..."

"Really," said Gloria. "Can I smell it?"

"Of course," said Dasha, "It's bees' honey and crushed woodland herbs. Only five pounds a bottle – in addition to the fortune-telling fee." She uncorked the phial and handed it to her eager client.

Gloria sniffed it gingerly.

"There's strange," she said. "I've never had scent like this before. It smells smoky."

"Smoky?" said Dasha. "Let me try!"

As she took the phial, however, a look of alarm spread over her face, and her nostrils twitched.

"Smoky!" she cried. "That's not the secret potion, there's a fire!"

And indeed, at that very moment a puff of acrid brown smoke drifted through a gap in the curtain, causing both of the occupants to cough. A faint crackling sound came from the direction of the kitchen.

"Oh!" cried Dasha, leaping up and instantly shedding her fortune-teller's demeanour. "There's a fire in the kitchen!"

She squeezed past Gloria, who had not had time to move, left the booth and darted over to the kitchen door. It was ajar, and smoke was billowing out.

86 — Mother Russia

"My rissoles must have caught fire," she thought. "It was the rum."

The situation, in fact, was just as bad as the smoke suggested. The fat and rissoles in the frying pan had caught fire and ignited some dishcloths, from where the blaze had spread to a shelf and the greasy walls. Even the bearded virgin icon was alight. Gloria followed Dasha in and looked past her shoulder.

"My Holy Virgin!" cried Dasha, staring at the icon. "Is there no end to our sorrows?"

It was already impossible to get to the kitchen taps. The best thing Dasha could think of was to grab a cauldron of rabbit borsch which, as it happened, was still within reach on the kitchen table, and throw it towards the blaze. This she did with an agility which belied her years. The borsch didn't damp the fire much, but it made an impressive mess on the floor.

"Where's Olga and Masha? And Trevor?" cried Dasha in despair. "I'm the only one here."

The fire was already spreading to the curtains.

"I'll call 999 on my mobile," said Gloria. "The fire station's only around the corner. They should be here quick to put it out. That's if they're not out on another job."

Her thoughts, however, did not match her utterance: "A lovely little piece for Swansea Day by Day..." flashed through her mind. "And if the blaze gets widespread, I could hit the front page! I'll have to get it in straight away, though, to catch the evening edition." She reached for her pencil and notebook.

Dasha ran to and fro, wringing her hands helplessly. Flames licked around the wall shelf, and eventually turned blue, doubtless on account of fumes from the

Chapter Three **87**

Captain Morgan beverage. Dasha must have spilt some when she handled the bottle a short while before.

"Can we get some water from the restaurant?" she cried to Gloria. "No," she said, answering her own question. "There's nothing to carry it in. Oh, I hope they come before it damages the fridges. One of them doesn't belong to us, anyway."

"Are you insured?" Gloria asked: it would be part of the story.

"I don't think so," said Dasha. "Olga would know that! Oh, God help us!"

On this occasion her appeal to the Almighty was successful, in so far as an impressive, red fire engine was just drawing up outside, its siren blaring loudly in the narrow Passage. A clutch of burly firemen, uniformed, helmeted, and heavily booted, tumbled out and rushed into Mother Russia. Two more began to unwind a light hose on the engine itself.

"In the kitchen, is it?" said one of them. "I'm George Dicker, the officer in charge. "Stove caught fire, did it? Same old story? Negligence."

He pushed his way in to survey the scene, and started giving orders.

"The small hose will be enough, Bert.... Bring it through here, will you, into the kitchen. Okay, give it a good squirt, now, to be sure that it's all out. And them smouldering bits."

A stream of water shot from the hose, soaking most of the kitchen, extinguishing the fire and trebling the mess that had to be cleaned up later. When the water was turned off, the firemen stood back to admire their handiwork.

88   *Mother Russia*

Officer Dicker turned to Dasha. "It looks as though a frying pan caught on fire, doesn't it? Was anyone in the kitchen when it started? Ah, what's this? A bottle of rum... spilt, I see. Above the stove. That may have contributed. If there's any negligence the council will fine you."

"Oh no," said Dasha. "I was only frying some Russian rissoles!"

"What do you put in them," asked George Docker, jovially. "Rum and aviation fuel?"

"Oh Jesus, you can be funny sometimes, George!" said the fireman with the hose. "Okay, stand back, it's not quite out yet. There's a bit still smouldering over there. Turn the water on again, will you?" (He obviously enjoyed his job.) "No electrics exposed, are there?"

"I presume you are the owner of the premises?" Officer Dicker asked Dasha. "We normally inform the police, and I'll have to do the usual report." He produced a form. "Name, address and contact telephone number, please."

"Oh, I'm not the owner," said Dasha, hastily. "I just help. You'll have to speak to my niece Olga Morozova and her friend Trevor Jenkins. They run it."

"Well, if they don't live on the premises you'd better give me their details," said the Officer. "But they'll have them down in the Guildhall, I expect... The police will be in touch with them.... You were lucky we came so quick. It could have spread further." He looked around. "Nice new fridge you've got there. Been spoilt a bit, hasn't it. Only the paint, though. Is it still working? Ah, I see it's padlocked. No matter. If it's not a fire hazard, it's no concern of ours. You know of course," he continued, "you'll have to close the restaurant until the kitchen has been refurbished. Then it will have to be checked by the environmental health people. There's a very decent man there called Mr Alberthwaite. He'll come and inspect.

Okay boys!" he called out, turning to his colleagues. "It's all over. We can get back to the station."

"Well, I'll be off too," said Gloria, who had observed the whole operation with keen interest. "I've got to get back to the office to write this up."

Dasha hardly noticed what she was saying: the erstwhile fortune teller was more concerned with her fees.

"That'll be eight pounds for the fortune-telling, she said. And five pounds for the scent. Thirteen pounds all together." Gloria fumbled in her pocket.

When they had all left, Dasha went back into the kitchen to view the dismal scene. "I hope the others will be back soon," she thought. "There's another little surprise for them!"

She looked at the Captain Morgan bottle of rum, and noted that it was now almost empty. She sat down for a moment and thought of her distant homeland. A tear welled in her eye.

"Perhaps we were better off in Verkhoyansk after all," she thought sadly. "Despite the communists, the snow, and the criminals."

The Evening Post building, as Gloria indicated, is but a stone's throw away from Salubrious Passage. The gulls perched on roofs nearby would have sensed the vibration of the printing presses as they filled the great reels of newsprint with matters of interest to the local citizenry. In his office the deputy editor, Gloria's boss, belched slightly on account of a chronic digestive problem, and looked at the first copy off the press.

90   *Mother Russia*

"I'm glad Gloria got her piece to us in time," he thought. "She's very good, really, and her history degree shows through."

He was familiar with the copy, but read it again. It read:

FIRE IN LOCAL RESTAURANT

Swansea's only Russian restaurant, "Mother Russia," located in well-known Salubrious Passage, was the scene of a fierce fire which broke out in the kitchen today. The circumstances of the blaze are not clear, but Miss Dasha Figova, one of the cooks, momentarily left the kitchen to attend an important interview. The alarm was raised when thick black smoke enveloped the premises. Dasha bravely entered the burning room and, regardless of the danger to herself, attempted to douse the flames with copious quantities of the restaurant's delicious borsch.

The services of the Swansea fire brigade, led by fire officer George Dicker, who arrived on the scene quickly, ensured extinction of the fire. Fire officer Dicker told the *Evening Post* that it could have been very dangerous. The older properties in the town are poorly fireproofed and, but for prompt intervention, the conflagration could easily have spread. Fortunately damage to the restaurant was restricted to decoration, some kitchen appliances, and a fridge. *Evening Post* readers with an interest in history will recall that the Great Fire of London, which devastated most of the capital, started in a small pie shop in Pudding Lane. So Swansea may have had a lucky escape.

The restaurant will be closed while refurbishment takes place. The culinary amenities will be greatly missed by Swansea's more adventurous gourmets, and we look forward to an early re-opening.

Chapter Three   **91**

We will not distress the reader with a detailed account of what happened when Trevor, Olga and Masha returned from the market: the recriminations, the anguish, and, on the part of the ladies, the tears. When Dasha admitted that she might have started it, after a glass or two of rum, Olga's anger was terrible to behold. Trevor stood back and allowed them to wage the quarrel amongst themselves, in their ineffable manner. But had Dasha not been so careless, and perhaps drunk, clearly there would have been no fire. When the outpourings eased, and all the emotions had been expressed, Russian fashion, Olga instructed the aged aunties to go home and have their afternoon naps and tipples. "Cleaning up," she said, "can be left until the evening: everybody needs a rest."

"And I'll have to discuss things with Trevor," she added.

So when all was at last quiet, and the door had closed behind the aunts, Olga and Trevor retired to the little office for yet another council of war. Olga could not but weep again.

"Oh, Trevushka," she sobbed. "Now we are really finished. The kitchen is burnt down, the Russian crooks have got us, the people in hospital may take us to court for poisoning, the environmental officer of health may not let us open again, there is no money in the kitty, and none of us have found husbands. It just couldn't be worse."

She made a number of expansive gestures – reminiscent of a badly played Lady Macbeth – and sank onto the red sofa. Trevor sat down beside her, willingly this time.

"Don't cry, Olga," he said, in fact quite tenderly. "Things aren't as bad as they seem. In a few days we'll get the restaurant going again. Perhaps that Ivan won't cause much more trouble, now that we've agreed to keep his fridge for him. It wasn't damaged very much. I'll play along with Fred Whopp, for a bit anyway, he may be

92 *Mother Russia*

queer but he's a decent chap. That is, as long as no one finds out. One bit of good news: yesterday I took out buildings insurance. With any luck it might cover the kitchen fire. Of course, we won't tell them that Dasha was tipsy."

"Oh, my little Trevushka," said Olga, perking up visibly. "You are so clever. So we won't have to pay anything to get it repaired?"

"I hope not," said Trevor. "As long as they can't prove negligence. But it will take a few weeks to resolve."

"What about the people who were poisoned?" said Olga.

"I don't think they will sue us," said Trevor. "If they know we're broke it wouldn't be worth the trouble. The main thing is the problem of keeping the business afloat in the meantime. I don't think we can depend on Dasha's fortune telling. She looks good, but there's not enough business there. She's only had one client in the week since we started. We need something with a much stronger appeal."

"What would that be?" asked Olga.

"Sex, of course," answered Trevor.

"Sex?"

"Russian sex. You must know a bit about that!" He gave her a playful push, but before she could respond he added, "A Russian massage parlour. Did you do any massage on the Volga?"

"Never," said Olga. "But some people went to a Turkish bathhouse."

"No matter," said Trevor. "You can learn. I'll get a couple of books on it from the library. If you do anything wrong you can tell people it's the Russian method. They won't know any better, will they? We'll have to advertise. People won't come unless they know about it."

"We could keep some leaflets in the restaurant," said Olga, uncertainly.

"Sandwich boards for Dasha and Masha," said Trevor, "in Russian peasant dress."

"Are you joking?" Olga asked.

And so the fate of Mother Russia was decided once again, at least in the short run. When the discussion was over, Olga cast a furtive glance at her business partner: "Men," she thought in her Russian way, "are so much more decisive than we poor women. Trevor is very manly! He'd get rid of Ivan Kravchenko, if he could. Thank God we have him here to support us!" She crossed herself, Orthodox fashion.

"I think I'll go back to the flat now," she said. "I feel exhausted. We can start cleaning up this evening. I'll send Dasha and Masha down. They'll have to do an evening shift."

"What time will they be coming?" asked Trevor.

"About seven, I suppose."

"I'll stay and make a start on it," said Trevor. "In any case, I have to look at the insurance papers."

In fact he wanted to be alone for a while, and think things over. After he had seen Olga out, he went into the office and settled down on the sofa. "Was this massage thing really viable, or would it be another flop? Could matters be arranged a little better? Some outside work for the old aunts, perhaps? The sandwich boards were a joke. And when Mother Russia reopened, how would things go?" He had tried to sound reassuring about the Ivan business, so as to calm Olga, but he felt far from happy about it himself. Any dealings with a petty criminal simply had to bring trouble. And what about this ridiculous fridge? They could not even look inside the damned thing.

He rarely slept in the afternoon, and his nights were now somewhat disturbed, but he felt as though he might benefit from a doze. And doze he did, under the dim *lampada* of the icon, for a good hour or more, until the daylight faded and the sea-gulls had retired to their craggy fortresses. All was quiet in Salubrious Passage.

He was awakened by the sound of another vehicle stopping outside. Peering through the curtains, he saw, once again, Ivan's cockle van. He anticipated a ring on the doorbell, but heard the click of a lock instead: he remembered that Ivan and his companions had a key to the premises. But something stopped him from coming out of the office – a feeling of unease, perhaps, an unwillingness to talk to Ivan or his associates. And why had they appeared at so unexpected an hour?

He opened the office door slightly so that he could watch without being seen himself. It was just Llew and Morgan. Since the restaurant was in darkness, they evidently thought it was deserted.

"Why don't they put the lights on?" Trevor thought. "They must be up to something."

The men were mumbling between themselves.

"The kitchen's back here, isn't it?" Llew asked his companion, nudging him forward in the darkness. "I hope no one opened the fucking fridge."

Chapter Three **95**

"They can't, they haven't got a key, have they?" said Morgan.

"The firemen may have broken into it," said Llew. "Or it may have got damaged. Ivan nearly went spare when he heard the place was on fire."

"Where did he find out so quick, then?"

"It was in the *Evening Post*. It mentioned a fridge had been damaged, too. I've never seen him in such a state."

"What happened then? Was any of the Ukrainians behind it?"

"No, one of the old hags started it by accident, and called the fire brigade. Ivan didn't want to come here while Olga and that bloke Trevor was here. He couldn't open the fridge if there was anyone around..."

At this point the two interlopers disappeared into the kitchen. Trevor decided to lie low – indeed, there was little else he could do. They might turn nasty if they found out he had been watching them: and there were two of them, anyway. Before long there were some grunting and shuffling sounds, and a swishing noise, as though something heavy was being dragged along the floor. The men came out of the kitchen, dragging what seemed to be a big plastic bag.

"Jesus, it's 'eavy," said Morgan.

"These Russian women got a lot of weight on them," said Llew. At least, that's what Trevor thought he said: Llew was panting heavily.

"Okay," said Morgan. "Wait here and I'll bring the van a bit closer." He went out.

"What does he mean?" Trevor thought. "What are they up to?" He looked closer: his eyes were now used to the darkness, and he experienced a tingling feeling in his

96   *Mother Russia*

spine. The contours of the bag, in so far as he could make them out, suggested a carcass of meat. The bottom was tied up with cord, but the bag was not quite big enough, and some of the contents protruded. Trevor could just discern a pair of red slippers on what might have been human ankles.

"Oh, my God!" he thought. "It's a corpse!"

Just then Morgan reappeared.

"I don't know why he put her in the fridge," Llew said to him, obviously disgruntled. "We've got to carry her everybloodywhere. He should have got rid of the body before."

"He didn't have nowhere to put it, did he?" his companion answered. "And he's trying to lie low after that business in Neath. He may be taking it with him tomorrow, when he goes down to Penarth. Perhaps he can dump it in the docks. The police will think she drowned. You can't get rid of a corpse all that easy."

"Well," said Morgan, "let's get it into the van, before anyone comes. Then we can go and have a drink."

The men raised their gruesome burden once more, and lugged it outside. Trevor heard the doors of the vehicle clang shut. But the reluctant porters had not closed the restaurant door, and a moment later they returned. They were evidently looking for something on the floor.

"Where is it then? Perhaps we lost one of her slippers."

"Are you sure there were two?" said Morgan.

"No, I'm not," said Llew.

"Well, perhaps it dropped off somewhere else."

"We can't bugger about with that now. It doesn't matter."

Chapter Three **97**

"You locked the fridge, did you?"

"Oh yes, there's a lot of stuff in it, what with the caviar and sturgeon. And another batch coming when Ivan goes down to Penarth, I think."

"What happened in Neath last week, then? Was you there?"

"Yes," said Morgan, "with a few of the others. And a good job, too. Ivan wouldn't have stood a chance by himself. There's a nasty crowd after him. Ukrainians, I think. They know he's turning a thousand quid a week, and they want to get in on the action."

"Well, you aren't doing too bad, either."

"This bloke, Dima, got in the way just as Ivan was going for a shave, and Ivan was a bit careless with his razor."

Both of the men laughed.

"Okay, let's be off, then."

They went out, this time locking the door behind them.

Trevor sank onto the sofa, overcome by what he had just witnessed. Whose body was in the bag? Was it one of the Ukrainians? What should he do? Inform the police? But he had nothing to show them! Would they believe him when he said that he thought he had seen a pair of feet sticking out of a bag, just for a moment, in half darkness? Had anyone been reported missing? Trevor had no means of knowing. And if the police thought there was something amiss they might suspect the restaurant was involved: the corpse had evidently been kept there. Olga was Russian and they would naturally think that she was helping a fellow-countryman. How could he, Trevor, and Olga actually prove that they had not known anything? And what about the restaurant business? If people found out that a dead body had been stored in the kitchen,

98 *Mother Russia*

nobody would cross the threshold again. And the small matter of the poisonings was still hanging in the air.

"I won't tell Olga yet," thought Trevor. "She would be terrified, and nothing has changed, really. Perhaps the best thing would be to try and persuade Ivan to bugger off and take his fridge with him? If he thought the police were suspicious he might disappear. What else is in it, anyway?"

He was engrossed in these dismal thoughts when the door opened again, the lights were switched on, and Dasha and Masha bustled in. Evidently they had come to do some cleaning, as Olga had mentioned. Trevor came out of the office to greet them.

"Good evening, girls!" he said. "Come to do some cleaning?"

"Life is toil, and old age is sorrow, as they say in Russia," sighed Dasha. "But what are you doing here at this time?"

"Just thinking," said Trevor. "Just thinking."

Chapter Four

(In which we observe amorous endeavours, albeit senile: the fridge losing part of its contents; and an unusual gathering in a grave-yard)

Emlyn Davies, a weedy little man, paused in Salubrious Passage and looked up at the sign above the great *matryoshka*: 'Mother Russia – Russian Food'. And below that, in the window, two smaller, newer notices. One of them, advertising psychic activities, is already known to the reader. The other read as follows:

OLGA'S RUSSIAN MASSAGE PARLOUR

Refreshing, Invigorating, Unforgettable

Genuine Russian Birch Oil used

Experienced Russian Masseuse

Apply within

"*Rwsiad,*" he thought. (He was a fervent Welsh nationalist, and disliked thinking in English.) "*Dyma'r lle yr oeddwn i'n meddwl amdano!*" And (we translate henceforth for those bereft of a knowledge of the ancient Celtic tongue) "I wonder whether she came here at all? Because she was Russian? The restaurant seems to be closed now. She wouldn't have gone to a massage parlour... But I'll give it a try. The people who work here probably all know one another."

100   *Mother Russia*

Emlyn pulled the brass doorknob, and heard a faint tinkle within. The door had a little Russian window, onion-shaped, cut into it, with a curtain. The curtain was moved aside for a moment, and Emlyn glimpsed a face peering out. The door opened, and he was confronted by a woman in her mid-thirties, slightly overweight, and dressed in a florid nightdress-like garment with a deep, plunging neckline. She had a red turban on her head and a brass chain around her ample waist. He guessed that this was indeed Olga, the Russian masseuse.

"Good afterr-noon," said Olga, with her usual Russian accent. "Come for a massage, have you?" She radiated a welcoming smile.

"Well," said Emlyn, hesitantly, in English. "How much is it, please?"

"It depends," said Olga, "on how far you want to go. There are various procedures." She paused, and decided from the visitor's modest, even shabby, appearance, that he was in the lower price range.

"Five pounds for a twenty-minute rub with soothing birch oil, followed by a hot shower, or..." – she paused, "up to twenty-five pounds for the full 'Volga' workover."

"What's a Volga workover?"

"It takes an hour. You get massaged all over, with a genuine River Volga mud pack for your neck and shoulders. Satisfaction guaranteed. Just like in Russia."

"Do you do a Tawe??" said Emlyn, attempting a little joke. "There's plenty of mud in that!"

"What's a Tawe?" asked Olga, equally curious. "Well, come in anyway," she added quickly. "We'll start you off, and you can decide what you want later. We'll see how things go."

Chapter Four **101**

Emlyn followed her in. He knew he would be embarrassed about the congenital red blotches on his back, but it would be worth paying five pounds, if he could find out what he wanted to know. He guessed that the masseuse would not mind a little dermatological blemish, provided it was not infectious. On one side of the restaurant a massage area had been curtained off: a stretcher-type couch stood in the middle, and little boxes with ointments had been set out on a side-table.

"What's your name, please?" said Olga. "I keep a register." Emlyn told her, and she wrote it down.

"No skin illnesses, I presume," she continued briskly. "Or anything unhealthy?"

"No," said Emlyn, "only a few blotches I've had all my life." Olga looked at them, unperturbed.

"That's all right," she said. "Just the occasional little ache or pain, is there? We can attend to that. Please get undressed behind the screen. Here's a towel and a Tartar dressing gown." She handed him a garment like her own, but without the cleft down the front. "Wrap the towel around you first."

"I didn't know Tartars wore dressing gowns," said Emlyn. "They told us in school that they rode horses across the steppes."

"You'd be astonished what they wear when they're at home in their yurts," said Olga. "I know, I worked on a tug on the Volga. It flows through Tartar lands. I saw a lot of them."

"Did you massage any?"

"Of course," said Olga. That's where I learned the ancient art."

102   *Mother Russia*

Emlyn disappeared behind the screen for a moment, and emerged in the long gown, having wrapped the towel around his middle underneath it. Olga gently opened the garment and sized up his anatomy. He was rather too white and skinny for Russian tastes. "But no matter," she thought, "as long as he pays."

"Oh, you could have a really nice body," she said encouragingly, "if you gave it the right treatment. Massage is very useful for people of your build. Lie on the couch and relax. I'll do your shoulders first."

As soon as Emlyn had comfortably reclined, Olga leaned over him, ensuring that her mammae were but a few inches from his chin, much as she had done with Mr Alberthwaite in the office. She began massaging her client's shoulders.

"How does that feel?"

"Very relaxing."

"When I was massaging the Tartars, I always began with the shoulders," said Olga in her sexiest voice. "And then I worked down."

"And how far down did you go?" said Emlyn playfully.

"Down to the payline," said Olga. "The world is the same all over, isn't it?" She began to finger Emlyn's rib cage.

"That's nice," said Emlyn. "But I thought you might be able to help me with something else, too... being Russian."

"What would that be?" Olga enquired.

"I'm looking for information about a member of our organisation."

Olga looked crestfallen: she had expected a slightly more intimate request.

Chapter Four **103**

"I'm from WFGST," Emlyn continued.

"What's that?"

"The 'Welsh Fallen Girls Support Team' in English."

"Oh, really," said Olga, still without the faintest idea of what he meant.

"We help local girls who are down on their luck," said Emlyn.

"I thought that everyone who lived in Wales was lucky," said Olga, thinking, "My God, he is skinny."

"Oh, by no means," said Emlyn, gently restraining Olga's hand, which had crept down as far as the edge of the towel, just above his navel. "A lot of Welsh people need help around here. We're an oppressed nation, you know. There are a lot of down and outs, homeless people, immigrants."

"Immigrants as well!" Olga nodded. That definitely struck a chord. "You help immigrants, do you?"

"Oh, yes. We're funded by the new Welsh parliament, see. The idea is to rehabilitate the unfortunates, and integrate them into Welsh society so that they turn into fine citizens... who speak Welsh, of course."

"What a good idea," said Olga. "Do you take Russians? I'd love to be turned into a fine Welsh citizen."

"Naturally," said Emlyn. "Almost anyone. Except the English. We've got too many of *them* already. Unless they genuinely want to convert."

There was a pause in the conversation. The thought of being a fine Welsh citizen was quite new to Olga; she had never been able physically to distinguish between the Welsh and the English, and indeed had never been bothered by a desire to do so.

104   *Mother Russia*

"I'll start your abdomen now, shall I?" she suggested.

But Emlyn was still pursuing his train of thought. He had not yet come to the point.

"In fact," he continued, marginally moving the towel to reveal more of his spotty belly, "I've come to ask you about a Russian immigrant."

"A Russian?" said Olga cautiously.

"I imagine you know lots of them. I'm looking for a Russian girl who has disappeared from the group we look after. She's gone without a trace. She lived down in Penclawdd somewhere, with some others. Do you by any chance know any Russian women down in Penclawdd?"

"Where's that?" said Olga.

"On the Loughor estuary," said Emlyn. "It's famous for its cockles."

Olga had heard enough – too much – about cockles over the last few days not to be on her guard. Ivan Kravchenko's disconcerting image came to mind.

"I don't know the place, or any women, either," she said. "Perhaps this one just lost interest in your classes. Or..." she added, "she found a good man to look after her." She massaged Emlyn a little harder.

"I don't think so. She was very keen on learning Welsh. If she intended to drop out she would have told me. Mind..." – he paused furtively – "She may have been an illegal immigrant. If they're regular attenders, we don't ask questions. If our numbers fall too low, the Parliament may stop our grant. She may have got mixed up with undesirables."

"What was her name?"

"Anna Petrovskaya."

Chapter Four **105**

Olga shook her head. "I don't know any Annas here. What did she look like?"

"About thirty, a bit fat, a sort of broad Russian face, blond. She wore bright clothes and a lot of make-up."

"I can't recall anyone like that," said Olga. "Certainly no Annas. Perhaps she called in one day when I was out, that is, if she came at all. My aunts may have seen her. They work in the kitchen."

"Can we ask them?" said Emlyn.

"They're not here just now, but I will, when they come back. Now let's get on with your massage. Don't be shy!" She pushed the towel down towards his iliac region.

Population statistics reveal (as the reader may be aware) that Welsh males are not lacking in reproductive potency. They have never been disconcerted by the traditional female use of blue flannelette drawers, and many, indeed, regard these unattractive garments as a challenge to their ego. At the same time, modesty has always been much prized – nothing disconcerts the average Cymro more than being fingered without his specific permission. The Russians lack such admirable sensitivity, so it never entered Olga's head that her client might regard his iliac as a no-go area. She was a little taken aback when Emlyn suddenly thrust her hand away, and tightened the towel around his waist.

"I think that will be enough," he said firmly, sitting up. "I feel much better already."

"Oh," said Olga. "I was just starting."

"I'm a bit short of time, too," said Emlyn, looking at his wristlet watch. "I've just remembered, I've got an extra class today. We're in the middle of '*bod*'. What a wonderful verb it is. How much will that be?"

"Eight pounds," said Olga.

"*Iesu Crist*," thought Emlyn in Welsh, "that's steep isn't it? She was only doing me for ten minutes."

But he said nothing, slipped behind the screen, emerged fully dressed, and paid the bill. "Better keep on the right side of her," he thought. "She might be able to help later. Or get us some new pupils."

He smiled.

"One small thing," he said. "If Anna does come here, could you let me know? I'll leave you my telephone number." He gave her a WFGST visiting card, and with that he was gone.

"I wonder whom he was talking about," thought Olga, as the restaurant door closed. "A Russian girl called Anna? Who lived in Penclawdd? Not another of Ivan's tricks, I hope."

Lunch-time arrived, and Olga went off to have her hair permed, using the takings from the massage. Just after she left the two aunts arrived. Trevor was not expected until later, so they had the kitchen to themselves. It was not long before the place filled with various sounds of culinary activity – the hiss of the gas stove, the bubbling of another cauldron of rabbit borsch, the sizzle of rissoles in the restaurant's ill-fated pan. There was also the slurp of sour cream as Dasha mixed a dollop of Russian salad. Although the restaurant was closed, pending another inspection by Messrs. Alberthwaite and Whopp, the kitchen was already perfectly usable.

Lunch today was a special occasion, for the aunts had arranged to do some entertaining. The table was carefully set for four, with bottles of Georgian wine and one of the

Chapter Four **107**

less expensive vodkas. Two benches decorated with Ukrainian motifs had been carried in from the dining room and placed at opposite sides of the table. A couple of limp roses, rescued from the restaurant before it closed, adorned the board. The celebratory atmosphere was enhanced by the ladies' attire – both had donned their Sunday best, comprising ankle-length black dresses which had been on sale in Perm' some three decades before. In fact, they had been the *only* dresses on sale in Verkhoyansk three decades before, which is why they were identical. Both Dasha and her sister were in a buoyant mood.

"I hope they'll like it," said Dasha, surveying the board.

"Oh, I'm sure they will...," answered the other. "Anything that's cooked with love... I'm glad you got to the dentist's, dear. You wouldn't believe what a difference a set of false teeth makes to your face."

Dasha bared her incisors and looked into a little mirror over the kitchen sink. In fact they were a little too large for her mouth, but that was intentional.

"I made the dentist give me ones that were a bit oversize," she said. "There's nothing makes a woman look more attractive than a good mouth of teeth."

At that moment there was a soft tap on the back door.

"Oh," cried Masha, with a little jump. "It must be them. I was sure they'd come."

"Who wouldn't?" asked Masha. "They know they're going to fill their bellies free, don't they?"

Dasha opened the back door a little, paused, and then threw it open wide.

"Welcome, welcome, come in, boys! It's all ready!"

108   *Mother Russia*

The guests were none other than Llew and Morgan, Ivan's henchmen. They entered rather sheepishly, as though they were visiting an old folk's home (which in a sense they were.) The hostesses had not had much of a chance to view them at close quarters before, but they did so now. Llew was a bit overweight, with a sagging midriff and balding pate; but he could manage a nice smile. His air of a determined, but beaten-up, boxer, did not, seemingly, disconcert his hostesses. Morgan was thinner, and his pinched features, even when he smiled, retained a hint of malign intention. But both visitors had made an attempt to dress decently in new jeans and expensive sweaters, so the overall impression was positive.

"Hullo, ladies," said Llew. "Very nice of you to ask us around."

"Oh, not formal," said Dasha, with a giggle. "Call us girls, not ladies!"

"The restaurant's closed down," said Masha, "but they can't stop us cooking for friends, can they? And healthy young men must have good food, mustn't they? Ivan hasn't come with you, has he?"

The two men looked at one another. "Well, no, he's rather busy at present," said Morgan. "I think he's got business in Penarth Docks." Llew unobtrusively stamped on his foot, but Morgan, being no less tough a character, hardly winced. Neither of the aunts noticed.

"Well, we thought you'd like to try a good Russian meal," said Dasha. "Ivan Ivanovich said that you would be coming sometimes to stock the fridge up."

They all looked at Ivan's large appliance in the corner.

"What's in it, then?" asked Masha, suddenly. "It can't be full of caviar and sturgeon."

The two men exchanged glances.

Chapter Four **109**

"Them tins takes up a lot of space," Llew ventured.

"Sturgeon is a big fish," added Morgan.

"Why does he keep it locked?"

"He told you. It's valuable stuff. So it can't get stolen. The Neath crowd might go for it. That's why you need protection, as well."

There was another moment's silence as the hostesses realised that they would get no further on that.

"Sit down, then," said Dasha, indicating the benches. "No, no, boys! Not both on the same side. Opposite one another."

The visitors did as they were told and looked approvingly at the festive board, particularly the bottled items. The aunts sat down as well, Dasha next to Llew, and Masha next to Morgan.

"You've got wine *and* vodka!" said Llew. "We both likes a drink."

"We know," said Dasha. "Who doesn't? No Russian will sit down to a meal without a *stopka* – that's a glass of vodka. Let me pour some out to start off with. You drink it down in one gulp, and eat some pickled herring straight after."

"In Russia we always propose a toast before we drink vodka," said Masha. There was a silence, and since neither of the men looked like responding, she raised her glass, and said: "To a long and happy friendship!"

The two men grinned, sharing, no doubt, the same thought – it can't be as long as that, not with two old crones in their sixties... But they all emptied their glasses, the crones with the ease born of long experience, the guests gasping.

110 *Mother Russia*

"Jesus!" said Llew. "We're not used to drinking shorts fast like that. We like to take our time and enjoy it."

"Eat something quick," cried Dasha, pushing the plate of herring towards them. "Have some salad as well!"

The two men dutifully did as they were told and, apart from some watering of the eye, were soon almost back to normal.

"It's so nice to have some friendly young men as guests," said Masha. "Normally it's just the three of us, with Olga, though Trevor comes sometimes. You live at home, do you? With your families?"

Had they been completely sober, the guests might have detected a slight tension in her voice.

"No." said Morgan, "We're both single, but we've had plenty of girl friends, like. We rent rooms."

Both Masha and Dasha seemed visibly to relax, their shoulders dropping slightly under the black silk of their antiquated garb.

"A little more herring, Llew?" said Masha. "Come on, you can manage more salad than that, a big man like you."

"I won the Neath weightlifting competition when I was seventeen," said Llew.

"You must have a wonderful appetite," Dasha was telling Morgan. "You're so athletic. Eat up!"

"I don't want to get fat."

"Fat?" said Dasha. "Fat? You've got nothing to worry about. You're all muscle!"

"I'd like to propose another toast," said Masha, this time rising to her feet. Dasha filled the glasses and looked at her expectantly.

Chapter Four **111**

"A happy family life for all of us!"

The two men looked at one another again: "How many more of these daft toasts would there be?" But they gulped the vodka down, and Morgan had the impression that his eyes were watering rather less.

"A warm heart is the most important thing in life," Masha continued. "A warm, loving heart close by."

The men tucked in to the cold *hors-d'oeuvres*.

"Rabbit soup next, boys," said Dasha, jumping up. Four steaming bowls of soup were quickly placed on the table. "*Smetana*, boys? Sour cream?"

"Sour cream?" said Llew, "I've never had sour cream. If it goes sour we throws it out!"

"It's lovely," said Masha.

Morgan suddenly felt Masha, who was sitting beside him, edge a little closer. A whiff of old-fashioned lavender, like the stuff his grandmother used to store clothes with, momentarily overrode the pungency of the soup. She turned her head and gave him a fleeting smile. He moved away ever so slightly.

"Go on, boys!" said Dasha, invitingly. "Propose a toast. The gentlemen are supposed to." Morgan nudged his companion. "Say something."

Meanwhile Dasha had filled the glasses again.

Llew, who had never made a speech in his life, raised his glass. "I would like to say thank you for this nice meal," he said. "And I hope we all have happy lives and that the restaurant opens again soon."

"Bravo! Bravo!" cried the two hostesses in unison. Morgan at the other side of the table felt a bit fuzzy, but he was sure he could sense Dasha's knee, a rather bony

Mother Russia

joint, pressing against his own. He looked at her in surprise, and she responded with a sly smile.

"We have talked about warmth and love," said Masha. "Let us not forget that one of the patron saints of "Mother Russia" was also the saint of matrimony – Saint Marina. Her kindly image has smiled upon many a ceremony at the Orthodox altar."

"Yes, many," whispered her sister, and pulled out her handkerchief to wipe her nose.

"Never heard of her," said Llew.

"Saint Marina was the ugliest girl in the village," Masha explained. "And she lost all her teeth in an epidemic of gum disease. She had never found a partner, and then, late in life, fell in love with a peasant who was forty years younger. He was short-sighted and wasn't worried about her features, but he loved her back. Unfortunately, one day when he was leading the cattle out to pasture, he mistook a randy bull for a cow and was gored to death. Marina was so upset that she became a nun, and specialised in consoling girls who had been jilted, or spinsters who couldn't find men."

"That's funny isn't it?" said Llew. "That sort of thing would never happen here. At least I never heard of a saint for jilted women. Have you, Mog?"

"No," said Morgan. "Most of them would be too ashamed to own up. Or they'd take you to court for breach of promise."

"As a matter of fact both of us were jilted," said Dasha. "That's why we are lonely. Our men were professional stove cleaners from Chelyabinsk. We told them we wouldn't mind them coming home all sooty. We were going to have a double wedding. But we kept them waiting too long."

Chapter Four **113**

"How was that?" asked Morgan.

"Our grandmother thought you should be courting for at least four years, otherwise people might think it looked rushed."

"In the end, they fell in love with one another, and eloped to Moscow," said Masha. "Mind, Chelyabinsk has got a name for that sort of thing... We were very upset."

"But we recovered completely years ago," said Dasha, looking at her sister.

"We certainly did," was the response, while the two men exchanged meaningful glances.

"Have you two got any girl friends?" Masha asked nonchalantly, as it were. "Have some more vodka, boys."

"No one at present," said Llew. "We've been away a bit, see, both of us."

"Oh, where?" asked Dasha. "On holiday?"

Both men burst out laughing. "That was no holiday," said Llew. "We was done for GBH, see."

There was a dull thud, and an expression of pain passed over Llew's face. Morgan had kicked him under the table again.

"What's GBH?"

"Er, Great Big Hearts," said Morgan. "We was helping the little kids at an orphanage."

"Oh, how kind. We both love children," said Dasha. "We often thought of adopting a few. We're a bit beyond having our own now." She gave a nervous titter. "But that wouldn't stop us getting married, though..." Neither of the guests seemed to react.

The meal proceeded apace and the alcoholic haze thickened. Neither guest, had they been asked afterwards, could have easily remembered what happened. Except, perhaps, the fact that the ladies insisted on being hugged and kissed on the cheek as they were leaving. Both females, despite their advanced years, were flushed and elated. Llew, for all his bulk, had a sentimental streak in his nature, and thought it all a little touching.

"Guess what?" he said to Mog, when the two men were safely out in Salubrious Passage. "I think they're after us. They must both be in their sixties."

"How daft can you get?" said Morgan. "I liked the booze and the rissoles, though."

Trevor had spent a sleepless night. Indeed, he could not remember ever having been so worried. The image of the black plastic bag being dragged through the restaurant, with a pair of feet trailing over the floor, returned a hundred times to his consciousness. He had tried counting sheep, making a determined attempt at self-hypnotism, and even recalling the hours he spent working for Swansea Sewers. Nothing had helped. So when his alarm clock rang at the appointed hour he was already uncomfortably awake.

Life had to go on, however, and in the course of the morning, while still at home, he directed his thoughts to some less disturbing, though important, matters, principally a re-opening date for Mother Russia. He managed to get Fred Whopp on the telephone at the Guildhall – Mr. Alberthwaite it seems, was out dealing with complaints about two Indian take-aways and a Turkish kebab parlour which had infringed the regulations.

"Good news," Mr. Whopp had declared. "Permission for re-opening Mother Russia will be considered urgently, in the course of the year. I've got it on the agendas of the relevant committees."

"Oh, I'm glad things will be moving so quickly," said Trevor in neutral tones.

"I've put it down for priority treatment as a special favour for you, Trevor..." There was a pause. "Pity you couldn't get along to *Hamlet* though, it was great! We're doing Milton's Paradise Lost next."

"And you've got someone to do Eve, I suppose?"

"Of course," Frank answered seriously. "Sinclair-Davies. He was so good as Ophelia."

Trevor left the house mid-afternoon (in fact while the aunties' little lunch party was in progress) and made his way down High Street, as usual. The weather had improved a little, and it was not raining. But the street had a sad, grey air, and the scream of the ubiquitous gulls overhead suggested unsettled weather to come. Trevor had not changed his mind about telling Olga of the body incident: better not upset her, especially as there was nothing specific to go on. But he had other matters to discuss with her – the news from the Guildhall, estimates for re-decorating, and the general prospects for his investment.

When he reached Salubrious Passage he passed Morgan and Llew on their way out. He greeted them with a nod, and was relieved to find that they were too drunk to talk. Olga, he found, had not arrived, while the two old women were clearing up in the kitchen.

"Where's Olga?" he asked.

She's gone to do some shopping," said Dasha. "She'll be back soon. Would you like something to eat? There's nice

116　*Mother Russia*

rabbit soup and rissoles." Trevor saw the pile of crockery in the sink and the glasses, and put two and two together.

"You've just had guests, have you?" he remarked. "Was it Ivan's boys?"

"Yes," said Dasha, "as a matter of fact it was. We asked them along specially."

"Specially for what?" asked Trevor. "They're not your type, are they, young men like that. And perhaps with a criminal record. I thought you were on the lookout for a couple of pensioners."

"What do you mean, not our type," said Masha. "We like all young men!"

"Anything they did in the past doesn't matter," Dasha exclaimed. "Nobody's perfect. In fact, they have been helping in an orphanage. They've got Great Big Hearts!"

At that moment Trevor heard the front door opening.

"Olga? Is that you?"

"Yes, Trevushka," said the familiar voice. "Sorry I'm late, my darling." She ran up to him, and kissed him on the cheek.

"How nice you smell this afternoon," he said.

"It's my new scent, all the way from Verkhoyansk. It's called My Pleasure. I'm glad you like it. But we must have a little talk about things. Oh, Aunties," she added, looking at the unwashed crockery. "You've had visitors!"

"Two," said Masha. "Those nice boys Morgan and Llew."

"Why did you invite them? The less we see of them the better."

"Did they collect anything from Ivan's fridge?" Olga asked.

Chapter Four **117**

"No, No. They just came for a meal."

Olga took her coat off.

"Okay, Trevushka," she said. "Let's go into the office. I have something important to tell you."

"Oh God!" thought Trevor. "I hope it's not another disaster."

He glanced at her face, but her expression was serene enough. He grinned, mainly as a way of concealing his unease. When they were inside she closed the door carefully, so that they should not be overheard, though there was little chance of that because the two aunties were busy discussing who was to have whom, Llew and Morgan.

"I had a visit from a man called Emlyn Davies today," Olga began. "He came for a massage. It was rather strange."

"What did he expect you to do?"

"Oh, nothing extraordinary," said Olga. "And I only charged him eight pounds. It was what he asked me that was strange."

Trevor waited expectantly. One of Olga's little foibles, he knew, was to make her listeners wait - if she had something interesting to relate.

"He was from the Welsh Fallen Girls' Support Team."

"What the devil is that?"

"They have some sort of grant to help down-and-out women, and teach them Welsh so that they can live in Wales as fine Welsh citizens. It's therapeutic."

"Can you imagine?" said Trevor. "All at public expense. But how does that concern us?"

118   *Mother Russia*

"I'm not sure that it does," said Olga. "But one of the women he was helping disappeared, and it caused a problem because they were below numbers in the Welsh class. Apparently this woman was a good attender, and he was afraid something bad had happened to her."

"Well, why should he come here, and ask you, of all people? I imagine people are dropping out of these classes all the time."

"He came here," said Olga, "because she was Russian. He thought I might know her. It's a Russian restaurant, after all."

"A Russian woman," said Trevor. A dreadful thought had flashed through his mind. Was it just a coincidence, or not?

"Did you know her?" he asked.

"No," said Olga. "He said her name was Anna Petrovskaya, but that didn't matter. We've not had a single Russian woman here that I didn't know. Certainly no Anna. She would surely have introduced herself to me. It's not something to hide."

"Unless she was an illegal immigrant. So you told him we didn't know her?" said Trevor.

"Yes."

Indeed, the more he thought about it, the fewer doubts remained in his mind: the pattern of events fitted together like a horror jigsaw, if there were such a thing. Per favour of Ivan, a corpse had been added to the situation, and then subtracted from it. For reasons best known to himself, Ivan had stored it in his fridge: perhaps because he thought there may be less of a problem with odours – the kitchen was quite smelly anyway. Indeed, the body may have been in the fridge when it was first delivered: the appliance had seemed suspiciously heavy.

Chapter Four **119**

Judging from what Trevor had overheard in the darkened restaurant, Ivan had probably panicked when he read about the fire, and decided that the corpse was best removed. Could it have been Anna's? Trevor realised that at this point he had to tell Olga all that he had seen and heard: Mother Russia was her business, after all.

"In fact," said Trevor dramatically, "I think she may have been here."

"Been here?" said Olga, puzzled. "You saw her, did you?"

"In a sense, yes," said Trevor.

"What do you mean, 'in a sense'? Did you speak to her?"

"No!"

"Why not?"

"Because she was dead when she came, and dead when she went."

Olga did not find it funny. She looked at him in silence, waiting for an explanation.

"Something very strange happened last night," said Trevor, "but I wasn't going to tell you, so as not to worry you. But after what you just told me things have moved on. What this Emlyn Davies said may explain it – up to a point."

Trevor then told her all that he had seen and heard the night before, including the plan to dump "it," whatever "it" was, in Penarth Docks.

"Are you sure you saw feet?" asked Olga.

"That's the point," said Trevor. "Not absolutely. But I think I did... the room was dark. It could only have been a dead body. They said, 'She's heavy'. There is a possibility that it was this Anna Petrovskaya."

120   *Mother Russia*

Olga's eyes opened wide with fear, and she breathed deeply, trying to control it.

"It all fits together, doesn't it?" said Trevor. "Otherwise it would be an impossible set of coincidences."

"Oh, Trevor, I'm really frightened now. Why is all this happening to us? With icons in every room, too. If only we could go to the police!"

"Well, we can't do that," said Trevor, emphatically, "not until your visa problem has been sorted out, anyway. And we can't prove anything. I didn't actually *see* a whole dead body, and it was dark. Going to the police would only make things worse. Even if it was a body, we don't know anything about it - was it a killing, an accidental death, or someone's deceased grandmother they couldn't afford to bury? Some people don't like spending money on funerals, they're expensive these days, you know. And she may have been an illegal immigrant as well. I haven't seen any report in the papers of a missing person. But if she was Russian, and no one knew about her, that's not surprising."

"This Mr. Davies did say one thing more though, didn't he?" said Olga. "He thought that Anna was one of a group of Russian women living down in Penclawdd."

"Well, here we are again," said Trevor. "Another strange coincidence. We're back to Ivan and his cockle business. He told us he's got premises down there, remember?"

"Why didn't he keep the corpse down there, then?"

We don't know what's down there, do we? Perhaps he wanted to keep the body for a few days, and he hasn't got a fridge there. Or maybe he thought Mother Russia would be more secure."

"It all gets worse and worse," said Olga, again on the verge of tears. "It's all because I can't find anyone to

Chapter Four 121

marry me, or Dasha, or Masha. If we had proper resident permits we could have gone to the police and told them everything."

"Well, it's not as simple as that either, with Ivan in the picture," said Trevor. "He could implicate us by telling the police we agreed to keep the corpse. And if the police didn't pick him up immediately he might come and do us up. Incidentally, Morgan and Llew were back today. I saw them in Salubrious Passage."

"Masha and Dasha invited them for a meal."

"Invited them for a meal?" said Trevor, incredulously. "Why was that?"

Olga thought it better not to answer: the amorous intentions of her elderly relatives were not something she wanted to enlarge upon.

"Oh, Trevor," she said. "What can we do now?"

"I think something we might try," he ventured at last, "is go down to Penclawdd and have a quiet look at the Cockle Company premises. It may all be above board and legal, but I doubt it. At least we might be able to get some idea of what's going on there. That might make things a bit easier."

"It can't be very legal if the manager has a razor in his briefcase and keeps a corpse in his fridge," said Olga.

"Indeed," said Trevor. "But hope riseth ever in the human breast."

At 8 p.m. that evening Trevor's slightly battered red Ford crept into Siloh Street, which was in fact just a double row of small terraced houses in the placid estuary village of Penclawdd. The vehicle was driven by its owner,

122 *Mother Russia*

the passenger seat being occupied by Olga. It was already dark and the streets were even quieter than usual. The only visible human activity was centred on the local fish and chip shop and two public houses.

"Do you know where it is?" asked Olga. "Ivan said it was an old chapel."

"Of course," said Trevor, slightly hurt. "I personally surveyed some sewers down here last year. They were in a pretty bad a state, too. People seem to throw everything into them. It must be the local mentality. There's only one disused chapel, and it's at the end of this street."

Siloh Street ended in a walled chapel graveyard, which was entered through a decorative iron archway. Trevor stopped the car in the middle of the street, some distance away, and they both got out, closing the doors quietly so as not to attract attention. The graveyard itself seemed to demand silence. Numerous headstones could be distinguished, a speechless army of memorials to pious souls long since disappeared. The visitors could feel a slight wind blowing in from the estuary, damp and shivery. Both felt uneasy in their mission: What would they find, if anything?

"I think I sense evil in the air," Olga whispered.

"Evil?" said Trevor. "No, it's just the cold air coming off the estuary. Or the corpses rotting. Graveyards aren't very happy places at the best of times... There's the chapel! And there's light in the windows! There must be somebody inside. Perhaps it's Ivan's lot."

"If it's a business," said Olga, "it's strange that they haven't got a sign up outside. Usually firms try and advertise."

Chapter Four **123**

"Well, let's have a closer look," said Trevor. "We'd better not go down the main path, somebody may open the door and see us. Better approach it from the side."

They made their way cautiously between the gravestones, contending with long grass, nettles and bits of crumbling masonry.

"God!" said Trevor, clutching his shin. "I've hurt my leg. I didn't see that." He sat down for a moment on someone's last home.

"Oh, Trevushka!" said Olga suddenly. "What's that?"

Trevor turned in the direction she had indicated, and saw two yellow spots gleaming in the dark.

"Haven't you ever seen cat's eyes?" he asked. "They always glow like that. They reflect any light there is."

And indeed the outline of a large feline, possibly a black tom, could be seen perching on a headstone.

"Perhaps we should go home," said Olga. "I don't like this at all. A black cat is a bad omen."

"No," said Trevor. "Not after we've come all this way. It's only the graveyard cat. It must live here. Seen quite a lot of passings, I bet."

"I didn't think we've be creeping through graveyards in the dark."

"We must have a close look at the chapel," Trevor rejoined. "You can go back and wait at the car if you want to."

"I'd rather be with you," she replied.

"Come on then."

The chapel itself was a modest stone building, probably Edwardian, with tall narrow windows. The sills were at shoulder height, and when the interlopers reached them

124 *Mother Russia*

they found that if they stood on tip toe it was just possible to see the dimly-lit interior.

"Look!" said Trevor.

An astonishing scene met their eyes. The polished wooden pulpit was occupied by none other than Ivan Kravchenko gesticulating expansively and eating fish and chips from a greasy paper. The few pews closest to him were filled with the sort of colourfully clad females who would not normally be found in sanctified surroundings. Some of them were eating fish and chips as well.

"My God!" thought Trevor. "Whores, one and all!"

Most of them did indeed look as though they had dressed for an intimate assignation with financial overtones. They wore make-up, mostly in copious quantities, with elaborate hair-does and plunging necklines. Some of the ladies were evidently tired, because they were resting their legs on the pews in front, revealing short skirts and shapely legs. A few of the shoes must have been hugely expensive, too. Some members of this unusual congregation were smoking, and one rather overweight lady, clearly visible to the interlopers, was taking surreptitious swigs from a pocket flask. Llew and Morgan sat in one of the back pews, engrossed in a game of cards. They could not understand what was being said, because it was all in Russian anyway.

"My God," Olga whispered, after a moment's viewing. "Would you believe it? And I know one of those girls."

Trevor glanced at her quickly.

"Really?"

"The thin one with blond hair, in the second row. Tanya Popova, the cook on our tug! I worked with her for years. She was offering personal services even then. Everybody knew."

Chapter Four **125**

Despite the tension of the moment, Trevor could not resist a brief quotation he learnt as a schoolboy.

"'The captain's daughter Mabel,'" he declared,

"'As well as she was able,

She gave the crew their weekly screw,

Upon the cabin table.'"

"Who's Mabel?" Olga looked puzzled.

"It doesn't matter," said Trevor. "A traditional English poem. I'll explain later."

Ivan Ivanovich had by now finished his meal and started to speak again. By a stroke of good fortune the window which Trevor and Olga were using seemed not to have been closed properly, so when Trevor gently pressed the wooden frame it yielded inwards. Voices became audible, speaking in Russian. Olga whispered the gist of it to Trevor.

"Nice these fried potatoes, aren't they?" Ivan was saying. "You got them down the road, did you, love?" He addressed one of the girls. "Has everyone paid up? We'll get some bottles of beer to go with them next time. Now let me see."

He pulled out a piece of paper from his pocket.

"I worked out a rota," he continued, "so that everyone gets a share of the best pubs, and does some time in the worst ones, too. It's got to be turn and turn about."

One of the women stood up.

"Yes, Nastya?"

"I don't think we should move around at all," she said. "The girls that have been here longest should have the best pubs. Then, as they find men and go off, other ones

126   *Mother Russia*

can take their places. There should be a queue, like in Russia."

"She's right," said another. "I've been here for six months, and I got a couple of regulars at the Plough in Treorchy. I think the blind one might ask me to marry him." A titter went around the chapel. "Why not?" she cried, looking around indignantly, "I'm a good hard-working girl."

"We all are," said someone. "It's a very demanding profession."

"The girls don't always move on," said another. "Sometimes they stay for months and months. Lena can't find anybody." The fat lady with the flask nodded vigorously. "So a rota would be the best thing."

"The Three Bears up in Velhindre is a good place," said another. "Very randy men up there. I don't know why."

The gathering became animated as the girls started comparing their sites.

"They're randy everywhere," said a big-busted blond. "You just have to know how to turn them on. I never have any trouble in the Hafod Inn in Swansea."

"Llanelly is terrible," cried another. "There was a man there who said he would give me thirty quid if I could let him have it the way he wanted it. 'What's that?' I asked. 'Ten quid down and a pound a week,' he said. He was short of money because he had to buy a coat for the missus."

"I'm sorry I came," said another. "There's not nearly as much money in it as I thought. I was talking about it with Anna the other day. She was disappointed as well."

Chapter Four **127**

"Yes," said another. "That's right. By the way, what happened to her? Anyone seen her recently? Did she get married?"

There was a sudden silence – the girls looked at one another questioningly.

"Where is she then?" someone else asked. "She hasn't gone back to Russia has she?" They all looked at Ivan.

"Anna?" he said, as though he were slightly surprised. "Oh, she decided to go back to Russia, her father fell ill and wanted her home to look after him. It was just like that..." He cleared his throat. "Now, as far as this rota is concerned, I'll draw one up so that everyone gets a share of the best pubs. It's the best way. How many are we servicing at the moment? Eight, is it? Now, can you pass this list around and see what you think about it, that is, without fighting. Okay? Now there's one other matter." His face lapsed into a broken smile. "Ira and Lena's icon studio. I already got the first lot back to Russia. It's a brilliant idea."

"How are they doing?"

"They've been selling well in the flea market in Verkhoyansk," said Ivan.

"There, I knew it," said one of the smaller brunettes. "They must be bringing you in a lot of money, Ivan Ivanovich, more than the cockles. So why haven't I had any of it?"

"Why haven't I had any?" said another girl, evidently Ira or Lena. "We do all the work! And it's cold in that bloody studio, too."

The other girl rose threateningly to her feet.

"Ivan, why don't you have it heated properly? Too mean? *You* wouldn't put up with it."

128   *Mother Russia*

"Don't you call me mean," said Ivan Ivanovich, obviously angry. "And how much I make isn't any of your business. I got you lot over, didn't I? You didn't have to come, you know."

Obviously a nasty row loomed. But just at that moment one of the girls looked over towards the window behind which Trevor and Olga were standing. Perhaps Trevor had inadvertently touched the frame again: in any case, a hinge had creaked.

"Get down quick," said Trevor, pulling Olga away from the sill. "I think we've been spotted. Back to the car!"

They ran tip-toe through the graveyard, and slipped out through the iron gateway. On reaching the street, they stopped and looked back over the cemetery wall. The door to the chapel had opened, and Ivan could be discerned standing in a shaft of light on the threshold: Llew and Morgan were just behind him.

A moment later the three men had plunged into the darkness of the graveyard, there were grunts and the sound of scuffling.

"Come on," said Trevor. "Let's get to hell out of here!"

He and Olga ran back to the car, and as they reached it a loud scream rent the air. Then, suddenly, all was again quiet. No one else, apparently, had heard it – at least, none of the denizens of Siloh Street appeared at their front doors. Trevor and Olga got into the car. The engine was warm and sprang to life immediately. As the vehicle moved off, both of them felt a profound sense of relief.

"What the hell was that?" said Trevor. Olga had grasped his arm again, and he could feel her shaking.

"Thank God they didn't see us," she gasped. "Let's get back to Swansea."

Chapter Four **129**

"Well," said Trevor, as they drove out of Penclawdd, "at least we've got a better idea of what's going on there. He's importing Russian women who can work the pubs, perhaps find husbands, and settle in Wales. But I wonder where that dreadful scream came from?"

"No idea."

"Well, just wait," said Trevor. "I'm sure there'll be a lot more developments."

And as the pages which remain might indicate, dear reader, he was quite right.

Chapter Five

(Olga meets an old friend, the Russian Orthodox church intrudes, and Trevor gets unusual employment)

A few days later the battered white van, now familiar to the readers, was making its way along the narrow road over a lovely rolling common just outside Swansea. It was one of those rare mornings when the sun was shining: a few wisps of cloud floated in God's heaven; a light wind wafted the scent of heather over the land, and the temperature was just right, evoking neither sweat nor shiver. It was one of those days, in fact, when it was perfectly safe to leave home without an umbrella, favouring the hopeless illusion that our normally rain-drenched Wales might emulate Tuscany. One or two rabbits hopped near the verge, well contented with their modest lot. All was green and lovely. It was also a working day, so there was no stream of tourist traffic to jar a driver's nerves. Motoring was a pleasure.

The man whose nerves might have been jarred was none other than Ivan Ivanovich, for it was he who, not surprisingly, was seated behind the wheel of the vehicle. In fact he was in an excellent mood, as indeed were Llew and Morgan, his immediate companions. Despite his protestations from the pulpit a few days before, his business ventures were going well. The Russian girls – currently crowded in the back of the van – were an attractive lot and likely to bring in a goodly sum before they found partners. Ivan would take a rake-off for protecting them. They were without any obvious signs of disease, and apart from a few on-going quarrels, appeared quite contented: Ivan could hear a reassuring murmur of conversation behind the partition.

132   *Mother Russia*

The icon business, though small, was building up nicely. The little fracas in Neath seemed to have blown over, the police having abandoned their investigation; all seemed quiet on that front. Apart from that, Anna Petrovskaya had ceased to be a problem. Her mortal remains still awaited final disposal, but they were carefully bagged and did not smell. After removal from the fridge, Ivan had hidden them under a loose gravestone in Penclawdd Cemetery, unobserved (he was sure) by any living creature except the cemetery cat. He had popped a piece of gravestone in the bag as well, so that it could be safely dumped in Penarth Dock when he next went down. Or somewhere like that.

"We'll be dropping the girls off at the same pubs, I suppose," said Morgan.

"Yes," said Ivan. "But Ksenia will be picked up by a man in the Nag's Head in Bridgend, near Seren Books. It's new ground. We'll all be calling in for a drink at Mother Russia's on the way. It's very convenient."

"Then we'll be collecting them tonight, as usual," said Llew.

"That's right," said Ivan. "The ones that haven't found men, that is. The others have got to find their own way back. They can spend a few pounds on taxis."

"How many have got hitched out of this bunch?"

"Two. One found an old rheumatic who can't walk, and needed someone to look after him, and the other got an unemployed police dog handler."

Morgan lowered his voice. "What did Anna do, really, then?"

Ivan peered intently through the windscreen, his relaxed mood gone. His features hardened.

Chapter Five **133**

"The fool," he said, as an impatient driver sped past. "He shouldn't have overtaken like that. I'd wring his neck... What?"

"What did Anna do?" Morgan repeated, rather hesitantly. Both he and Llew had had experience of Ivan's anger.

"She got involved with some charity that was helping the poor," said Ivan. "Like the charity kitchens in Russia. She said she wanted me to change things, and give the girls a better deal. She threatened to go to the police. So I changed things..."

Neither Llew nor Morgan needed to ask anything more. There was an uneasy silence. A hint of recklessness crept into Ivan's driving.

"Careful," said Morgan. "You nearly hit that cow."

"They shouldn't have let it stray."

"So we go to Mother Russia's first?"

"Yes, I've arranged to call in there. I have to put one or two things in the fridge."

The others looked down and, for the first time, noticed a plastic pouch lying on the floor of the van.

"The takings, Ivan, is it?"

"No business of yours," said Ivan. "You get your screw, don't you?"

There was another moment of tension.

"The girls can get out and have a drink when we get there," said Ivan, by way of a diversion.

"I thought it was closed on account of the fire," said Llew. "We was invited there for lunch in the kitchen. There was a notice up."

134   *Mother Russia*

"This is a private arrangement," said Ivan. "They'll be waiting."

An amateur version of 'Moscow Nights', a popular Russian melody, broke out behind them: the girls were feeling musical.

"Not bad at all, is it?" said Morgan. "The singing, I mean. I've never heard that one!"

The van proceeded on its way – down the leafy Mayals with its posh houses, along the broad, open road behind the bay, past the great white Guildhall, then through some of Swansea's meaner streets. Eventually it pulled up in Salubrious Passage.

The three men jumped out and approached the door of Mother Russia. Ivan had a key, but he pulled the bell knob, nevertheless. After a moment the little curtain swished back, and Olga's face appeared behind the glass. She was by no means pleased to see the visitors. She half-opened the door.

"Oh, hullo, Ivan Ivanovich," she said. "We didn't expect you!"

"Didn't you know we were coming?"

"No," said Olga. "I think you must have spoken to one of my aunts. They didn't pass it on. The restaurant is closed. But come in anyway."

The three men edged their way in.

"Any chance of a few drinks?" said Ivan, surveying the empty premises. "I've brought some friends, as I told your aunt. A few ladies. They're immigrants from Russia, and they're doing wonderful work picking cockles in Penclawdd. You must have a few bottles somewhere? Yes, there they are," he added, looking at the restaurant rack.

Chapter Five **135**

"Plenty of wine and beer left. Call the girls in, Morgan, it's their little treat."

Morgan went out and dutifully opened the back door of the van. The ladies, freshly made up, and as garishly attired as ever, clambered out. None of them had been to Salubrious Passage before, and they looked with interest at the quaint archway and facade.

"Okay, girls," said Llew in a loud whisper, intended to be inaudible inside the premises. "Free booze. It's a Russian restaurant. And you're all picking cockles in Penclawdd, Okay?"

"What are cockles?" said Ira.

"Poor man's oysters," said Morgan. "They live in shells buried in the sand. They love it. Come on."

Olga held the door open and watched helplessly as a dozen or so of her countrywomen filed in. Some gave her slight nods.

"There's Tanya Popova," she thought. "I wonder what she will do when she sees me?"

By now Ivan was busy pouring drinks at the counter. Tanya, as it happened, was the last person to enter. On catching sight of Olga she stopped dead in her tracks.

"Olga," she said, glancing furtively around, "What are you doing here?"

"What are *you* doing here?" Olga responded.

Visibly shaken, Tanya went up to collect her drink, and was lost for a moment in the crowd. By now everybody was talking and drinking: Dasha and Masha looked on through the kitchen doorway, smiling and trying, though in vain, to catch the eyes of their chosen cavaliers. In fact, they were supposed to be washing the kitchen floor. Llew and Morgan were just downing their third glass of wine

136   *Mother Russia*

and seemed mildly embarrassed, trying to avoid the beatitudinous smiles that were flashed at them. When Tanya emerged from the crowd, she saw Olga surreptitiously beckoning to her. Olga slipped behind the curtain which encircled the massage area, and Tanya followed.

"What's going on?" said Olga. "Who are these girls?"

"Street girls from Verkhoyansk," said Tanya. "Ivan got them over."

"And what are they doing in Swansea?" Olga asked innocently.

"It's Ivan's prostitution racket. He advertises in the Urals newspapers for girls." Tanya recited something she evidently knew by heart: 'Who would like an exciting career at a lively British holiday resort, girls with poise and artistic ability particularly welcome. Entry into the UK with accommodation and a residence visa assured. And for the most talented, sure matrimonial prospects.' It's a big fraud. Everyone who's here fell for it."

"Why the Urals?"

"Fewer questions asked than in Moscow, the girls are more naive and more anxious to get to Europe. There were hordes of us trying to get in on it. Ivan interviews you and charges $3,000 for everything. But when you get to Britain you find you're smuggled in, you're an illegal immigrant, and you daren't tell anyone. Otherwise get imprisoned or sent back to Russia. Ivan gives you a bed in the Penclawdd Methodist Chapel, and you have to pretend to work in his cockle business. In fact, you're a call-girl looking for customers in the South Wales pubs. He takes a big rake-off from what we earn and keeps tabs on all of us. We depend on him because most of us don't speak English and haven't got anyone else to turn to."

Chapter Five   **137**

"So how does he get you into the country?"

"On a sea-going tug from Amsterdam," she replied, "up the Bristol Channel. And then you get loaded into his cockle van and brought down here. In the dark, of course, so that no one can see."

"Well," said Olga, "there are quite a few of you. Can't you all stand up against him together?"

Tanya gave her another frightened look. "There are three of them," she said. "Not only Ivan, and they can be violent. Only one person has been able to get away so far; that was Anna Petrovskaya. We don't know what happened to her, though. No one has heard from her since."

Olga looked at the frightened face before her. Should she tell Tanya the dreadful truth? Or would that make her even more scared? Too late, the moment had passed.

"And we think it's going to get worse," Tanya continued. "There's this struggle going on with the Ukrainians in Neath. Ivan hasn't said anything, but we think he's trying to break into their drug market. We would have to be the couriers. But thank God it hasn't started yet. That would be really dangerous... I'd better get back to the others," she added hurriedly. "Ivan might notice. He's taking us out for the night's work. Then he'll come and pick up the ones who have finished, and take them back to Penclawdd. Olga, if only I could get away from him! Can you help me?"

"I will if I can," Olga replied. "But I'm not at all sure. I haven't got a visa myself, you know, neither have Dasha or Masha. And Ivan says he's..." – she paused meaningfully – "'protecting' Mother Russia. In fact he keeps a big fridge here. He won't tell us what's in it."

There was nothing more to be said: Tanya's appealing look was to remain in Olga's memory for many a long year afterwards. Olga followed her back out into the restaurant, though waiting for a moment so that they should not be seen together. Ivan was in a jovial mood again, and pouring out another round of drinks. Some of the girls crowded around him for topping up, while others sat at the tables, talking, drinking and smoking. A game of cards had started in a corner, and occasionally a shriek of unmistakably whorish laughter rent the air.

"Drink up, girls!" Ivan exclaimed. "It's on the house! Oh, I almost forgot..."

He picked up the plastic pouch he had brought with him and made for the kitchen.

"Just got to put something in the fridge, Olga," he said. His hostess thought this might be a golden opportunity to see what he was keeping in it, and made to accompany him.

"No, no," he said. "No help needed. I won't be disturbing anyone, will I?" He slipped into the kitchen and closed the door behind him.

The familiar smell of pickled vegetables and gas leaks struck his nostrils. With the noise of the party blocked out, the kitchen seemed strangely quiet. He chuckled as he pulled out the keys. "Good idea using this place to keep things safe," he thought. "Very convenient. No problems with the Neath crowd, either. Now let's see, which key is which?"

Given the quiet, he had not thought to check for any other human presence. But human presence there was, though invisible to him: Masha and Dasha were there on their knees, washing the floor behind the kitchen table. Seeing a pair of male legs appear, Masha peeped over the top of it. Ivan was just opening the fridge door, and Masha was able, for an instant, to see the contents. Then Ivan, having placed the pouch inside, closed the door, locked it, and went back into the restaurant. Masha sat up on her haunches, puzzled.

"Did you see inside?" asked her sister.

"Just for a moment," was the reply. "There were some plastic bags on the top shelf, a cash box, some fish, I think, and a few tins of caviar…"

"Anything else?"

"Some women's clothing," said Masha. "And icons."

"Icons?" said Dasha, in amazement.

Back in the restaurant, Ivan looked at his watch: it was time for them to be off.

"Okay, girls," he cried. "We'd better move on now. Enjoyed your drinks, did you? Let's get back into the van! Llew, Morgan, come on. Thank you, Olga," he added, with a rare display of courtesy. "See you soon!"

The van drove off, and the restaurant was suddenly empty again. Olga looked around at the tables which needed to be cleared of dirty glasses and ash trays. The old Russian saying flashed through her mind once more: 'An uninvited guest is worse than a Tartar.' A saying that went back to the time of the great Tartar invasion in the twelfth century. "As true as ever," she thought.

Masha and Dasha emerged from the kitchen.

""They've gone, have they?" said Dasha. "And those lovely boys, too?"

"What lovely boys? I didn't see any."

"Morgan and Llew."

Olga grimaced.

"What do you think?" Dasha broke in excitedly. "Masha saw what was in the fridge. We were in there when Ivan opened it."

"What was there? Tins of caviar?"

"Not only," said Masha, and repeated what she had told her sister.

"Icons?" said Olga, at first no less surprised. Then she thought for a moment. "Icons... Yes, Ivan had said something about icons when he was talking to the girls in the chapel."

"Oh my God!" she thought. "He's using Mother Russia for his icon business as well."

And to her aunts: "Well, we'll have to see what develops," she said.

The hours immediately after Ivan's visitation passed with some profit. There were two massage clients, a burly docker and a thin little man from Tesco's, and both seemed satisfied with the service. Olga had extra reason to be pleased, because both of them had found out about her from a small advert she had placed in the *Evening Post*. But as her fingers ran contentedly over the relevant anatomies, Olga's mind kept on returning to Ivan and his fridge. "Caviar and cash, yes...but icons? Silly, wasn't it? Even a corpse fitted the existing pattern better. The gang seemed to lack any spiritual aspirations, but you could never be sure. Perhaps they went to church on the sly? Trevor would be puzzled, too, when she told him. The

Chapter Five **141**

Ivan Ivanovich problem seemed to get ever more complicated as time went by. God knows," she thought, "what will happen next."

She did not have to wait long to find out, in fact only until about four o'clock. The Tesco employee had just left, after making another booking. Olga had gone into the kitchen to ask her aunties to make her a cup of coffee. When she returned she casually glanced out of the window, and saw, to her astonishment, two gaunt, black-robed figures standing outside, looking at the signboard. Their beards and soft black hats confirmed their calling as Russian Orthodox priests. One of them was carrying a shapeless shopping bag, and Olga recognised him as Father Varfolomei, the priest who had officiated at the Russian birthday celebration.

The doorbell tinkled, and Olga went to open it.

"Good day and bless you, Olga," said the good Father. There was a certain softness in his voice which belied his forbidding mien. His companion smiled.

"Oh, fathers," said Dasha, quite overcome by their arrival.

"This is Arch-priest Grigorii," said Father Varfolomei. "You remember we met at that lovely birthday party you had here a few days ago."

"You are very welcome," said Olga, getting a grip on herself. "Do come in and sit down. Would you like some tea? I have some lovely wild strawberry jam, with strawberries from the Russian woods. Our tea is Georgian. My Aunt Dasha can make pancakes in a few moments if you so wish. Auntie Masha, Dasha," she called out. "We have more visitors."

"A glass of tea would be very nice," said Father Grigorii, "but nothing else, thank you."

142   *Mother Russia*

Three chairs were placed around one of the restaurant tables, while the aunts, who had emerged from the kitchen for a moment, greeted the priests, crossed themselves and went back to do the tea.

"I wonder why the hell they've come here," thought Olga, as they took their places. "Perhaps they saw the notice in the *Evening Post*, and have come for a massage. Or to complain about it. As a matter of fact I've never done a priest. I imagine they get quite flabby about the waist."

The priests, however, were in no hurry to reveal their motivation, let alone their anatomies.

"It is always a great pleasure to find little corners of Russia in other lands," said Father Varfolomei. "The ladies here are all Orthodox, I imagine?"

"Oh, yes," said Olga. "We were all christened. We have a lovely icon of the virgin of Tobolsk watching over us as we toil in the kitchen. What a pity there is no Orthodox Church in this part of Wales."

"Well, there aren't enough believers to have one," said Father Grigorii. "As yet. Perhaps one day, when there are more Russians living here..."

"We've got too many already," thought Olga.

"Do you have many Russian customers?" was the next question.

"Very few," said Olga. "There's a gentleman called Ivan Ivanovich who is involved in the cockle trade, some ladies in the service industry, and some people in Treorchy, but that's about all so far. Most of our customers are local people. We are trying to introduce them to our wonderful Russian cooking."

Chapter Five **143**

"An admirable endeavour," said Father Varfolomei. "Borsch, *smetana*, rissoles, mushroom pie, I suppose."

"Possibly caviar and sturgeon, too," said Olga.

At that moment Masha reappeared carrying a tray laden with an ornate teapot, a little electric samovar, glasses, saucers, and individual dishes of jam. She put the tray carefully on the table and began to set the tea-things out. Dasha came to help. The priests looked on approvingly, and there was a pause in the conversation. Then the clerics exchanged glances: the time had come for them to explain the purpose of their visit.

"There were one or two things we might ask you," said Father Grigorii, "since you are good Orthodox souls..."

The two aunts simpered, while Olga attempted a devout smile.

.".. with no hint of ungodliness in your natures."

"Certainly not!" said Masha.

"No hint of it!" cried her sister.

"Well, the first thing is this," said Father Varfolomei. "Our mother church in London likes to keep contact with Russians throughout the country. Safety in numbers!"

"Strength, strength, not safety," Father Grigorii chided him. "We are all safe enough in God's hands. We like to think that our church presence is well felt among our countrymen, even though they may not have occasion to attend our services. Tell me," he continued, "do you have any room for storage, I mean a cupboard, or something?"

The image of Ivan's fridge drifted ponderously across Olga's mental horizon. "Storage! What exactly would they be leaving, anyway?"

144　*Mother Russia*

"Well, we're rather short of space," she rejoined. "But what would you want it for?"

"Just a few packets of leaflets about our church and our activities, something which your Russian customers might be interested in," said Father Varfolomei. "And a small display stand. We have some Russian bibles which are distributed free, as well."

"I'm sure we could find a corner for that," said Olga, with some relief. Irrationally, she had anticipated another fridge. "The only thing is, the restaurant is closed at present, and we don't have any Russian visitors. But if you would like to leave some material... I can see how things go and contact you."

"Wonderful," said Father Grigorii, pulling out a sheaf of leaflets and a few smart new bibles from a small bag. "This little stand folds up, you see. May God bless you, and your worthy establishment. But there was another thing, too."

Suddenly he became very serious, and, sensing yet another problem, Olga's heart fell.

"We have a dreadful instance of ungodliness to solve. Incredible though it might seem... Oh!"

He buried his face in his hands, and rather unthinkingly wiped his eyes with the edge of his cassock.

"Father Grigorii," said his companion. "Don't grieve so!"

"I'll be all right in a moment," said the older man. "Let me have a sip of tea."

"You see," said Father Varfolomei meaningfully. "He's so upset about it. He's got heart disease. He nearly passed away the last time he was so upset. Shall I explain it to them?" he asked Father Grigorii.

Chapter Five **145**

"Yes, yes," was the answer. "You tell them." Father Grigorii fumbled under his robes and brought out a bottle of lurid green pills, one of which he swallowed forthwith. "I'll be all right now."

"The Patriarchate of All Russia," said Father Varfolomei, "is very concerned about unhealthy new trends in youth culture in Moscow. It may spread to other large towns."

"Loose living, sex outside marriage, homosexuality, moral decay..," said Father Grigorii.

"Disrespect for the Orthodox Church..," added Father Varfolomei. "Alcoholism, divorce..."

"Marriage is a fine institution, father," cried Dasha, "and should be strongly encouraged!"

"At any age," Masha added.

"And not allowed to fall into decay," said Olga.

The whole company was quite carried away by the unanimity of their views, and for a moment a sort of elation reigned. The fact that none of the laity present had been to church for decades did not seem to matter.

"I'm glad you have such Orthodox Christian attitudes," said Father Grigorii. "Perhaps you have information which might help us get to the bottom of a new and evil trend."

"And what trend might that be?"

Father Varfolomei rummaged in his bag again, pulled out another small packet.

"I can't bear to look," said Father Grigorii, blinking a little.

"This is what we mean!" said Father Varfolomei, removing the paper. The icon underneath it was, at first sight, brown with age, and the three ladies craned

146　　*Mother Russia*

forward to look. Closer inspection, however, suggested that it was lacquered to make it look ancient.

"God forbid," said Masha, crossing herself again, Orthodox fashion. "Look at that."

Everyone gasped. The Madonna depicted in the icon had two oversized breasts, almost as large, relatively, as Olga's, but with exciting, blue nipples. The Madonna herself had been endowed with a slightly sexy smile.

"And this one," said Father Varfolomei, "is worse!"

The second icon depicted a gaunt, venerable saint holding a candle in one hand and a slightly bent dildo in the other. There was a hint of a grin, possibly queer, on his face. Be that as it may, both icons could not but be acutely embarrassing to any right-thinking Orthodox believer. None of the ladies could find anything to say.

"Yes," said Father Varfolomei dramatically, dropping the offending images back into the shopping bag. "Lewd icons! Probably the first ever in the thousand-year history of the Pravoslav church." He wiped a bead of sweat from his brow, and took off his soft black hat.

"These icons were bought in a bazaar in Verkhoyansk," said the priest. "In fact there's a whole rash of them. They're trickling into Russia from abroad."

"Throughout the land," repeated father Grigorii, weakly. "Sacrilege! Even in Soviet times, there was nothing like this."

"Terrible," said Olga, as another dark thought crossed her mind: Ivan again? "But how do you think we can help, down here in Swansea?"

"A local product," said Father Grigorii. "One of the icons had initials and a tiny place name painted on it."

Chapter Five **147**

He retrieved the Madonna from his bag and turned it over. "Lena Sergeeva, Penclawdd" was painted in minuscule letters in one corner. The inscription had evidently been added at the whim of the artist, and could hardly be discerned.

"And," Father Varfolomei added, "Mother Russia is about the only place in Swansea where we were likely to find Russians."

"Can you help us?" asked his fellow priest earnestly. "Do you know anyone who might be involved? Where's this place Penclawdd? Fighting this evil is particularly difficult for us, because these horrible things are being produced abroad. If it was in an artist's studio somewhere in Russia, the church could track them down and act through the local militia. But here we are almost powerless."

There was silence: Olga's mind was racing, while the two men of God looked at her intently. "This must be Lena and Ksenia's work," she thought. "Church pornography for dirty-minded believers! It was what the girls were doing in the chapel studio, between their amorous appointments. And there was a pile of it in the fridge, too. Once more, it all fitted together." The question was, should she tell the priests what she knew? No! Again she had no real proof. She could not tell them what she had overheard at the chapel window, or what Masha had – apparently – seen in the fridge. It couldn't be opened, anyway. And other consequences? What if the priests went to the police? Blue-painted tits were no great deal in this day and age, but any police interest in Mother Russia was – given all that had happened – to be avoided.

"Perhaps they were indeed painted in Swansea," she said. "Penclawdd is a village not far from here. And I only know a few Russians. But if we hear anything at all, we will certainly let you know. Can you give us an address I can write to, or a telephone number, here or in Russia?"

"The Embassy in London is best," said Father Grigorii, recovering his composure a little. "Or the Patriarchate in Moscow, though letters take a little time. We have to get to the bottom of all this. Is there anybody else we should see down here? Our holy task is to minister to those in spiritual need."

"I know, I know," said Olga. "There must be many people who would welcome you, as we have done. I don't have any addresses, though."

"Well," said Father Varfolomei, "we know there are a few families scattered around, mixed marriages, mostly. But I don't suppose there's much more we can do for the time being."

The two men rose to their feet.

"Bless you for any help. We have told you what the problem is, and rely on you to keep your eyes and ears open. We shall get the five o'clock train back to London, and remember you in our prayers."

Olga accompanied them to the door and watched them make their stately, though somewhat incongruous, way down the Passage. She sighed. Some more bad news for Trevor, she thought. More trouble to be avoided.

Trevor, at that moment, was in fact much concerned with other matters. Swathed in an old sheet, a towel wrapped around his head, he was balanced on a flimsy step-ladder, painting the cracked ceiling of his living room. One good thing about the passing of the older generation, he thought, is that it allows you to get on with jobs which were impossible before. He'd been trying to get this done for years, but his mother always stopped him.

Chapter Five **149**

He dipped his brush into a large tin of paint, and drew it carefully over an as yet untouched corner.

Painting always brought out the philosopher in him. "Women," he thought, pausing in his endeavours, "are strange creatures. Dad always used to say that man has three problems with them – getting out of one, getting onto one, and getting away from one. Olga? She seems very keen on me at present. A bit too much, really: she'd have me in her bed like a flash, if she could. I won't mind, either... the only thing is, it might give the wrong signal. I do like her. She's obviously sensible underneath, but sometimes I think she's a bit too showy, not my type. I suppose her weight could come down. But in my more reflective moments, when I'm painting ceilings, for example, I realise I must stay my hand, not to mention my other parts. And she's after a visa as much as a man. Mind, I reckon I've done her a favour by putting my capital into the business. Not to mention trying to keep on the right side of Fred Whopp. "Oh, hell!"

His exclamation was directed not at the council employee, but at the worn carpet beneath him which was rapidly absorbing a small pool of white paint which had fallen from his brush. He jumped down from the ladder and grabbed a wet rag. At that moment, however, the telephone rang. "It can't be Olga," he thought. "The restaurant is closed." He picked up the receiver.

"Hullo!"

"Is that Mr. Jenkins?" It was a man's voice, unknown to him.

"Speaking!"

"This is Fred Parker, Area Manager of Swansea Sewers Ltd."

150   *Mother Russia*

Trevor felt uneasy. Swansea Sewers. There was only one thing they could be ringing about: not another sewer job?

"How can I help?"

"I gather you did some work for us last year, re-mapping the network. And you have some experience of work below ground."

"Yes, that's right," said Trevor.

"Well, we've got an urgent problem, and we wonder whether you can help us out. There's a major blockage in Penclawdd, and the workmen there have to be supervised for an hour or so. It would be on a one-off, commission basis."

An immediate decision was called for, but Trevor hesitated.

"Just one thing," the voice added. "We'll shortly be having a vacancy in the mapping and surveying department. All above ground, of course. You'd probably have a good chance of getting it, if you were interested..."

"I can be there in half an hour," said Trevor. "There have been blockages there before, I believe. Penclawdd people seem prone to them."

"Come to Nolton Street, then, where the blockage is. We'll be expecting you."

Trevor replaced the receiver, picked it up again immediately, and dialled Olga's number.

"Olga?"

"Is that you, Trevushka?" The rich tones were unmistakable.

"Yes. Now look, I won't be along to the restaurant this afternoon, because I've been called out on an urgent job. A blocked sewer in Penclawdd."

"Oh, Trevor," said Olga. "Work! How lovely for you, my little goat. But when you come down here I have something more to discuss with you. We've had some more unusual visitors."

"More?" said he. But perhaps she only wanted to gossip about her massage customers. It could wait.

"You can tell me later, I'll certainly be along."

"Is it a big, big job," said Olga, "for ever?"

"No, just for this afternoon. But I can't miss it, they may offer me something permanent."

"Well, come back as quickly as you can when you finish, Trevushka," she said. "Something else has happened."

Trevor freed himself from his unusual garb, stuffed his waterproof working clothes into a canvass bag and went out to the car. On that occasion it started without difficulty, and he arrived at Nolton Street half an hour later. Fred Parker, middle-aged and business-like, was waiting for him. He was already attired in his waterproof sewer gear and gave an impression of total competence in matters of urban evacuation.

"Glad to meet you," said Trevor. "It must be about a year since I was here last. I don't think we met then, did we?"

"I've only been here a few months," said Frank. "I was promoted from Crosshands. Everything has been rather quiet so far, except for today. The most inconvenient time, just when we're having the All-Welsh Knitting Exhibition in Cardiff."

"Oh," said Trevor. "You have an interest in matters sartorial?"

152   *Mother Russia*

"No," said Frank. "I just like clothes, or more precisely, knitwear. I've got a scarf and two pairs of socks in for judging. But this is a serious blockage, and it doesn't look as though I will be able to get up there in time. We've called the police in to stop the traffic while we're underground. They should be along soon. I've never been down that tunnel myself and I wanted to have someone with a bit of experience go with the gang. Brought your waterproof stuff, have you? Can you get changed in your car?"

Trevor donned his own waterproof garb, and by the time he had done so some policemen arrived and started to cordon off the area, causing some traffic congestion. A manhole cover was off and a few locals were waiting to see what was happening around it: very little ever happened in Penclawdd, so any incident attracted attention. A couple of policemen and some sewer-men were also waiting there, with pumps and ladders, ready to start work. Trevor greeted them and looked down into the dark aperture: it reminded him forcefully of the day he had been bitten by a rat.

"There must be a couple of feet of sludge there," said Frank. "And it's backing up fast. If we can't clear it soon, it will flood the street. And then we won't be able to get down there at all."

There was a note of urgency in his voice.

"Okay," said Trevor, authoritatively. "I think it must be blocked at the junction of A34 and C12. Very unusual for anything to get stuck at a big union like that. But with sewers you never know."

"If someone has misused the drains," said Frank, "Penclawdd Council may prosecute. That is, if they can find who done it. It could be a major health hazard. You can't let people get away with that sort of thing. It can't be

Chapter Five **153**

normal issue from the outfall drains, somebody must have lifted a manhole cover and dropped something big down. Builder's rubble, perhaps. Highly irresponsible, that's what it is."

"Get the ladder down, then," Trevor told the sewerman. "Then we'll have a look. I'll go first."

He leaned over and gazed into the smelly depths, trying to accustom his eyes to the darkness. The sludge was almost immobile, but one sensed it was creeping ever higher against the old Victorian brickwork. Trevor had his foot on the first rung of the ladder when a sound of a car caused him to look up. One had just driven up at speed and screeched to a halt at the police barrier. Prominently displayed on the windscreen was a notice: PRESS – *Evening Post* Reporter. Trevor glimpsed a woman's face behind the windscreen. Gloria Evans (for it was she) jumped out of the vehicle and smiled warmly at all present, which is what reporters always do when they sense a good story.

"Hullo folks," she proclaimed breathlessly. "I'm Gloria Evans from the *Evening Post*. Call me Gloria."

"Oh God," thought Trevor. "That's the girl who did the fire story. She's come complete, no doubt, with notebook and camera."

Somehow or other, Gloria knew him. Perhaps she had seen him working at Mother Russia. And she knew his name, too.

"Oh, hullo, Trevor," she said, catching sight of him. "You're in on this as well, are you? Didn't I once see you at Mother Russia? Dressed up as a peasant?"

"I did this work before," he answered, "for a short time."

"Lovely to see you again. The office had a call from a local resident: he said the drainage system had broken

154   *Mother Russia*

down and extensive flooding was anticipated, with a red health alert and a possible cholera epidemic."

One of the policemen grinned.

"Oh, things aren't nearly as bad as that," said Frank. "We've just got an unusually bad blockage, that's all. Flooding is a long way off."

"Oh, I'm sure it won't be that long," said Gloria with a hint of pleasurable anticipation in her voice. "After all, if a main sewer is blocked..."

"I suppose you want to see the whole area submerged in shit," said Frank expressively. (He didn't like to have inexperienced newspaper reporters poking into his professional concerns, and despite his gentle passion for knitwear, he had a coarse streak in him, too.) "It would make a better story, wouldn't it?"

"Do you know what caused it?" asked Gloria, ignoring the remark. If there were no crisis, how could she write a big story? A run-of-the-mill piece about sewers would never reach the front page. It was too distasteful, and most of the readers would be too old-fashioned to see the funny side of it.

"No, we're just beginning the investigation," Frank answered. "These gentlemen are just going down to have a look."

"You *will* speak to me when you find out, won't you, Trevor?" Gloria pleaded. "I'll give you a good write-up. News is a bit thin today."

Trevor nodded his assent, and turned his attention to the job in hand. He clambered down the manhole, followed by the workmen.

"All right, Trevor?" Frank shouted, when he had disappeared from view. "How deep is it?"

Chapter Five **155**

Trevor switched on the sewer-man's lamp he had been given, and all of a sudden the secret subterranean world was brightly illuminated. Human shadows showed up black against the stained, orange walls.

"Up to two feet, I imagine. But shallow enough to wade through."

"It's pretty nasty, boys," he added, turning to the others. "If the smell gets worse we might need masks. Pity I used my best after-shave this morning, it's wasted down here. No rats as yet, but they can't be far off. Whatever's blocking it can't be more than twenty yards or so further along. There are ledges sticking out at some of these junctions, and they can cause trouble. We might need some prods or dragging equipment. Come on."

He gestured with his free arm and the little band moved bravely forward.

"Jesus, the stench! It's getting worse," someone said.

However, they were nearly there. A few yards further on some dark bundled objects could be perceived, sticking up above the surface of the unmentionable.

"There it is," said Trevor. "A pile of something has got jammed against that brick column. What can it be?"

He approached it gingerly, followed by the workman, and directed the beam of his lamp towards it.

"It's some stuff in sacks!"

Rubber gloves were part of the sewer equipment, so Trevor was able to use them to grope under the surface of the sludge... "No, surely it couldn't be!" With growing horror, he felt what seemed to be a human arm, a shoulder, and then a foot, all detached, and (as mathematicians say) discrete. A second foot, and then a

156   *Mother Russia*

third! There must be a second torso to go with it! Trevor struggled to control his revulsion.

"It's dead bodies, boys!" he gasped. "Dismembered!" And then, he added, "Two, I think. But I didn't feel any heads. Can someone hold the lamp?"

He forced himself to lift a piece of something above the surface, just to be sure: no doubt about it, it was certainly the stump of a neck and shoulder, covered with black sludge. Two sackfuls of human remains! No wonder the drain was blocked. He felt queasier than ever and wondered how his companions were taking it. But they were all experienced sewer-men, and this was no time for wimpish frailty.

"We'll have to get it all out," said Trevor, recovering from the initial shock.

The three of them together eased the heavy sacks back, and the sludge in the tunnel, freed of restriction, surged forward, almost sweeping them off their feet. But the level dropped to a few inches, which made things easier. There were in fact three sacks, not two.

The workmen grabbed them and dragged them back to the manhole.

Frank Parker was looking down through the aperture, waiting for news.

"Found it?" he asked. "I see the level's dropped back. What was it?"

"Dead bodies," said Trevor. "Dismembered."

"Dead bodies?" said Frank. "Oh, my goodness! How many?"

"Two, I think... in sacks."

Chapter Five **157**

"Good job the police are here," Frank exclaimed. "They'll have to get an ambulance or something to transport them to the morgue. For identification."

"I not sure they'll be easy to identify," said Trevor, "in that state."

"Why not?" said Frank.

"No heads," said Trevor. "At least, I couldn't feel any."

Frank turned a shade greyer, his face almost matching the colour of the lovely lambs-wool cardigan he had knitted for himself.

"Perhaps we'd better keep it all down there until we get something to put it in," he said. "Plastic bags, or something. A lot of people have gathered here now. Some of them might be upset."

Gloria's face was the next to appear in the bright circle of sky. She had, of course, been listening intently.

"Dismembered bodies!" she exclaimed, scarcely able to conceal her excitement. "Trevor, this is big, big. It'll run nationally, no, world-wide. Pity I haven't got a photographer down, but the police probably wouldn't allow him to take pictures. We'll have the manhole photographed, though. Where's my mobile?" She started looking in her bag.

"Could you stand back, miss?" Trevor heard Frank's voice behind the barrier. "Constable, can you come and have a look?"

"What a way to end up," thought Trevor, surveying the filthy sacks. "A short while ago they were living human beings, with full lives in front of them. They couldn't have been here for more than a day or so, though, or the sewage level would have risen more. How did they get there? Murdered, decapitated, and dumped upstream.

158 *Mother Russia*

Perhaps something will come out in the autopsy. I wonder, I wonder..." He recalled Ivan's unpleasant visage.

Fortunately the sewer-men did not have to wait long in their dark surroundings. Penclawdd is a small locality, and the sound of an ambulance siren was heard within a very few minutes.

"There's not much point in them rushing," thought Trevor. "This lot isn't going anywhere."

There followed a police request to pass the filthy sacks up through the manhole. By the time Trevor and the workmen got up to the street, the malodorous sacks had been put into large plastic bags ready for dispatch to a local morgue. Frank Parker had recovered his composure somewhat.

"A terrible business," he said to Trevor, as the ambulance moved off. "I didn't expect anything like this. I suppose the police will try and find out where it all went down. They'll want to see the sewer maps. Good job we had them updated."

"We'll have to have a contact number for you, sir," said a sergeant, approaching Trevor. "I believe you're the person who actually located the bodies. We've got to have the autopsy and identify them. You may be required to make a brief statement."

Trevor gave the policeman the particulars usual in such cases.

"The manhole cover can go back on, I suppose," said Frank, making a gesture to the workmen. "It's all been quite quick. I think I'll be able to get to the judging in Cardiff after all, the last part, at least. This will be in the papers, will it?" he added, turning to Gloria.

"You bet," said she. "Definitely a front page story. I'll be writing it myself."

Chapter Five 159

"I'd better come back to your office, Frank," said Trevor, peeling off his sewer suit. "I must give you an invoice."

"And then," thinking to himself, "it's down to Mother Russia to see what's been happening there. The ceiling will have to wait."

At Mother Russia Trevor anticipated a warm welcome, some considerable surface contact with Olga, and smiles from the old aunties. He would tell them the startling tale of the human remains in Penclawdd, and take some sly pleasure, perhaps, in their horrified reactions. If the truth be told, he was savouring the Russian reactions in advance. Though it was not something to joke about, of course. But Olga got in first.

"You'll never guess what happened here this afternoon," she said, as soon as he came through the door. Dasha and Masha had come out of the kitchen to enjoy his surprise.

"You'll never guess what happened in Penclawdd, either," said Trevor. "You tell me first."

"Well," said Olga. "Many things. Ivan brought the girls here for a drink, on us, of course - the whole lot of them, and I was able to have a quick word with Tanya Popova. It's an illegal call-girl business, all right, but it isn't going very well. The girls are terrified of him, but they're here without visas and they've got nowhere to turn. I feel really sorry for them. I don't know what I can do to help."

"We've got too much on our plate already," said Trevor.

"Then there was this icon business," Olga continued. Trevor looked at her questioningly.

"You remember some of the girls complained that they were cold in the icon studio? When we were listening at the chapel window? Well, this afternoon, completely out

160   *Mother Russia*

of the blue, I had a visit from Father Varfolomei, the priest who was at the Russian family party, remember? He came with a Father Grigorii from the London diocese. They are trying to build up an Orthodox congregation in the provinces, but they were doing a bit of detective work as well. So it was two things – the icons being made in the chapel are lewd, and the Orthodox Church is trying to find out who makes them."

"Big deal," said Trevor.

"That's not all." Olga leaned closer. "They had heard that a Russian girl called Anna had gone missing, and asked me if I knew anything about her."

"Anna, Anna," said Trevor. "So priests are looking for her as well. The whole thing seems to get worse by the day!"

"Tell us what happened in Penclawdd, then, Trevor," said Olga.

"You'd never believe it," he replied. "The main sewer was blocked by three sacks of human remains. We think there were two dismembered corpses."

All three ladies were visibly shocked.

"I've never seen anything like it. Stomach-churning. I had to get them out, with some workmen to help.

"And how did the bodies get down there?" said Olga.

"They don't know yet," said Trevor. "Two people were obviously murdered, perhaps the murderer couldn't think of any better way of getting rid of them. He probably thought the bits would be washed out to sea."

"Murder again!" interrupted Olga. "Do they know who it was?"

Chapter Five **161**

"How could they?" said Trevor. "They were in sacks, very dirty, and there weren't any heads."

There was another stunned silence.

"The police said it would take time to investigate," Trevor continued. "No one has been reported missing yet..."

The same painful thought, of course, was in everyone's mind – there was already one unclaimed corpse in the locality. But two? And close to Ivan's Chapel?

"It couldn't be..." said Olga.

"Ivan again!" Trevor completed the sentence. "Perhaps he's been in another brawl. Thank God we're not involved in THIS, anyway," said Trevor. "I never really saw Anna, and we don't know a thing about her. So we just keep our heads down and hope it will all blow over. The sewer story should be in tomorrow's *Evening Post* – believe it or not, that reporter Gloria Evans turned up to cover it. Remember, the girl who did the story on the fire? She was thrilled. They don't seem to miss much. Mind, I could benefit from it myself. I didn't get claustrophobia, and there's a chance that Swansea Sewers will offer me a mapping and surveying job on the basis of it. But the sooner we get shot of Ivan and his bloody fridge, the better."

Both the aunts jumped up and gesticulated wildly.

"Certainly not," said Dasha.

"We can't get rid of that fridge," cried Masha. "If the fridge goes, the boys will stop coming."

"The boys?" said Trevor, unable, for a moment, to grasp what they were getting at.

162   *Mother Russia*

"They're trying to get themselves married to Llew and Morgan," Olga explained, matron-like. "I thought you knew."

"At their age?" said Trevor. "They've left it a bit late, haven't they?"

"It's got nothing to do with age," said Masha indignantly. "It's affairs of the heart. They're very nice boys. They like us. Age doesn't matter."

"No, but visas do," said Olga. "That's what you're after."

"You're trying to do the same thing yourself, aren't you dear?" said Masha with an unpleasant leer. "You'd grab anything going!"

"Don't judge other people by your own terrible standards," said Olga, just as nastily. The conversation was taking too intrusive a turn. "Finding nice men is a little easier if you are in the younger generation, though!"

"All right, girls," said Trevor, rising to his feet. "Cool it! The way things stand at present we can't possibly get rid of Ivan or his fridge. Let's all have a nice glass of Russian tea."

Chapter Six

(A ladies' day at the beach, disturbing news, and a visit to a police station)

The following morning dawned fine and sunny. Trevor went down to the restaurant earlier than usual – indeed he was there before eleven. Olga and the aunts were discussing, in their usual heated manner, a new menu for when the establishment re-opened, although there was no immediate prospect of it doing so. The argument centred on whether the caviar should go in at eight or twelve pounds a portion. The fact that they could not get at it, and no one would buy it anyway, was lost from view. When Trevor walked in, smiling, they were glad of the diversion.

"I think what we all need," he said brightly, "is a few hours by the sea. To mark our new start. The weather has improved, and if we're lucky it might not rain all day. The water shouldn't be too cold for bathing, either. It's August."

There was an enthusiastic response.

"Oh," said Olga. "I haven't been swimming for years. Dasha, Masha, you'd like that too, wouldn't you?"

"We've both got swimming costumes," said Masha.

And so it was decided to spend the afternoon at Caswell Bay. An hour later, Trevor was driving his ageing Ford into the parking area for visitors. It was Saturday and it seemed as though half of the town had decided to visit this, one of the most popular, spots in Gower. The whole area was crowded. Lightly-clad families cheerfully unloaded the appurtenances of beach living from their cars – folding chairs, ice boxes, inflatable toys, and audio

164   *Mother Russia*

devices guaranteed to shatter any vestiges of peace that lingered on the littoral. The girls in Trevor's car – more exactly, the three not-so young females in Trevor's car – were all in excellent spirits. The dark events of the last few days had somewhat receded from their minds.

Olga got out of the car first, followed by the aunts, one of whom was clutching a large, ungainly shopping bag with towels and bathing costumes sticking out of it. The other carried a plastic picnic basket. Their dress was definitely 'vacational': Olga had donned an extraordinarily vulgar floral frock purchased God knows where; Trevor had noticed that though she was not overly interested in clothes, she tended to go for things that were revealing and flamboyant. The two aunties were in distressing pea-green, Stalin-era creations, high collared and calf-length, clearly drawn from their antediluvian Verkhoyansk wardrobe. Trevor, in shirt-sleeves and grey shorts, looked positively drab in comparison.

Out of the car, the Russians filled their lungs with the salty air and looked up at the cloudless blue sky, as holiday-makers do everywhere. There was a happy anticipation of a relaxed, if noisy, afternoon.

"Don't forget to lock the car, Trevor," said Olga. (She had a propensity, Trevor had noted, for giving instructions.) "Look at that wonderful beach, and the blue sea beyond. Paradise. A marvellous idea to come here."

"It's a bit crowded," said Trevor. "In fact, it's bloody packed."

"Not compared to Russia," said Masha. "The beaches on the Black Sea get really crowded. You have to get up at six in the morning to find a place to lie down. If you come later you have to sun-bathe standing."

Chapter Six **165**

"And then you get people complaining that your shadow is keeping the sun off them," Dasha added.

"It's never as bad as that in Caswell," said Trevor. "Usually there's no sun. Off we go, then. Have we got everything we need?"

The colourful little party picked its way between the parked cars, over a roadway jammed with traffic, and down to a beach filled with sprawling adults and frolicking children. A few hardy young males, clearly just out of the water, were shivering and rubbing themselves with towels.

"Cold, is it?" Trevor asked one of them.

"Bloody freezing," was the reply. "You gets used to it, mind."

"There's room here!" said Olga.

They paused at a small area of sand left between two large families talking animatedly in Welsh. The Slavs and Celts looked at one another with a common curiosity.

"*Albaniaid ydynt nhwy,*" said someone in the Welsh camp. "*Galwchl eu gweld hwy yn hob man.*" There were uncomprehending smiles on both sides.

"There's plenty of room for us here," said Trevor.

"Shall we have a little snack to begin with?" asked Masha, as they settled on the sand.

"What have you brought?" asked Trevor. "It's lunch time."

There was a clink of crockery as Dasha fumbled in the basket. "There's some lovely rabbit soup – it's nice cold as well – and rissoles."

"Not the ones that were left over when the kitchen caught fire?" Trevor asked.

166   *Mother Russia*

"I've scraped all the burnt bits off," said Masha defensively. "They keep in the fridge all right."

A brief, uneasy silence followed, broken by the cries of children and the intrusive throb of a portable stereo. The word "fridge" had a special significance for all of them, recalling, as it did, Ivan, Anna and all the other problems they had brought.

"About that fridge," said Trevor, rather impulsively. "They haven't been back to take anything out, or put anything in it, have they?"

"No, no," said Olga. "Not for several days now!"

"Well," said Trevor, with a shrug. "There's nothing to be done about it at the moment. I don't want any cold rabbit soup, thank you, but I wouldn't say no to a rissole."

"And some lovely black bread and pickled cabbage," said Dasha. "Masha, get the plates out, will you?"

But Masha was fumbling with a big black leather binocular case.

"A Russian soldier I knew brought these binoculars back from Germany," she said. "They're wonderful. You can see for miles."

And indeed when she got the appliance, with its black leather and bulging lenses, out of the case, the others could not but admire.

"I was told," said Masha, flourishing it, "that Rommel used these glasses to view Stalingrad in the distance. He looked through them with his own eyes."

"Just imagine," said Trevor. He thought Rommel had been in Africa, but he wasn't too good on German generals.

Chapter Six **167**

"They're incredible glasses," Masha continued. "You can see everything close up!"

She swept the horizon, capturing inside the bright optical circle a container ship off shore, the limestone cliffs topped with greenery, and the populous beach world around them. Suddenly, inside the brass eye-pieces, her eyes narrowed. A group of familiar figures had come into sight.

"Good heavens!" she cried. "I can see some of those Russian girls, the ones who came to the restaurant."

"Are you sure?" said Olga.

"Yes, in bathing costumes. They must be having a day out as well. And wait a minute, there are men with them!" She gave a little gasp of excitement. "It's those lovely boys, Llew and Morgan."

"Let me look," said Dasha quickly.

"I haven't finished yet," said Masha, fending her off with her elbow. "Oh, and Ivan Ivanovich too."

"Give me those binoculars," said Dasha, making another grab at them.

"Oh no you don't!" said Masha. "They're mine." A small tussle started, somewhat to the amusement of the indigenous crowd sitting close by. Granny fights were not in the Welsh tradition.

"Why are they always fighting about things," thought Trevor. "Stop it!" he shouted, jumping up. "We don't want any scenes here, we'll be the laughing stock of the beach. Masha, give Dasha a turn."

Masha yielded the glasses reluctantly, and Dasha looked through them.

168   *Mother Russia*

"They're so muscular," she said admiringly. "They've got up, now. They're in yellow swimming trunks, magnificent... Yes, they're going into the water. They've got those breathing pipe things."

"Snorkels," said Trevor.

"Come on Masha," said Dasha hastily, the question of nourishment completely forgotten. "Let's go for a swim. Where are our costumes?"

Olga extracted from the bag two cover-all swimming suits, again identical and hopelessly outmoded, but this time pink in colour. The ladies fussed over the towels and rubber swimming caps, and changed into the costumes as fast as they could. Then, oblivious to the stares of their Welsh neighbours, they tripped down to the water, leaving Trevor and Olga to keep camp.

When they reached the water's edge they found a slight swell, and some rollers. It looked fun.

"It's freezing," said Masha, as they waded in.

"I don't think so at all," said Dasha. "If your circulation is bad, dear, it's probably the drink. But it's too late for you to do anything about it at your age."

"Cold water will do your varicose veins the world of good," her sister retorted. "They look rather bad today."

They both gritted their false teeth and waded deeper against the oncoming waves. Within a few moments, they were far enough out to be able to swim, or more accurately, flop about. When they had got used to the cold they stood up and looked around. "Where were the muscular snorkellers?"

"Can you see them?" said Masha.

"Yes, there they come."

Chapter Six **169**

The old ladies watched appreciatively as two yellow bottoms bobbed through the foaming water, propelled by strong legs and flippers. Both Dasha and Masha positioned themselves carefully so as to be within grasping distance when they got near.

"Let's give them a little surprise, shall we?" said Dasha.

Just as the snorkelers reached them, their heads still under water, Dasha smacked the bottom closest to her, while her sister followed suit with the other. Both swimmers sank, re-surfacing and spluttering a moment later. Then, as though Fate had so decreed, a slight surge swept the ladies forward, each onto her own snorkeler; and with that all four went under again, the ladies clinging to their prey. When they had all found their feet, panting, and chest-deep in the briny, the ladies gave contented, if washed-out, smiles.

"Hello! You didn't expect that, did you?" said Masha.

The swimmers removed their snorkels and looked at each other: they certainly had not.

"I think she tried to grope me while we was under water," Llew said to his companion.

"Well, it makes a change, doesn't it?" said Morgan.

"Lovely swimming trunks, you've got," said Dasha. "I've never seen yellow ones before."

"We was both in the Neath swimming team," said Llew.

"Come down for the afternoon, have you?" asked Dasha.

"Well, we're just keeping the girls company," said Llew.

"And seeing they don't go astray," Morgan added, with a wink.

"That's nice for them, isn't it," said Masha. "Two fine, strong men like you!"

"If you've got time, we could go for a little drink," said Dasha. "There's a booth near the road."

As though by instinct, Dasha and Masha grabbed Llew and Morgan firmly, an arm each. The two men did not, in fact, need much urging: after several unsuccessful visits to the betting shop, they were a bit short of cash. A few quick beers at the old aunts' expense would not come amiss.

"Okay," said Morgan. "Very nice of you to invite us, just what we need after our dip. We can't be too long, though. Ivan wants to get back to Penclawdd fairly early."

"I'll go and get some money from my bag," said Masha. "I won't be a minute. I'll see you up there." She waded towards the beach.

When she got back to their little patch, she found Trevor eating alone. He looked up.

"Where's Olga?" she asked.

"She's gone for a swim by herself," was the answer. "I'm keeping an eye on things till she gets back. She won't be very long. What are you looking for?"

Masha was delving into her bag.

"Money," she said. "We've invited Llew and Morgan to have a beer."

"Llew and Morgan again?" said Trevor. He turned aside so as to conceal a wry smile.

Meanwhile, however, Olga was having a little adventure of her own. She had looked through the binoculars, and

Chapter Six **171**

also found reason for a quick swim: Tanya Popova was in the water with the other girls. This might be a good opportunity to have another word with her. Olga's swimming gear was of genuine Marks and Sparks provenance, so she attracted less attention than her aunts as she made her way to the water. Shivering, like everyone else, she waded out towards the Russians. When the water was breast-height she started swimming herself. Now she could hear the women calling out to one another. She could not see Ivan – apparently he had not ventured into the water, but she located her old friend and swam towards her.

"Hi, Tanya!"

Tanya, who was treading water, glanced around, and then swam to meet her.

"I would never have expected to see you swimming off the Welsh coast," she exclaimed, in a feeble attempt at a joke. "We've all come down for the afternoon."

"I was expecting you to telephone me," said Olga. "I gave you the number."

"No chance," said Tanya, fearfully. "The phone at the chapel is locked up, it's not easy. I did try from a bar, but no one replied."

"So what's going on? Any developments since we met?"

"If anything, things have got worse. But I don't want the others to see me talking for long. It might get back to Ivan." She glanced towards the shore. "In the last day or so, Ivan's got very irritable. Either he has problems with the Ukrainians, or something else happened. And we think he's been in another fight in Penclawdd."

"What makes you think that?"

172   *Mother Russia*

"A few nights ago we were in the chapel, discussing the bars with Ivan. Suddenly he jumped up and rushed outside. I think he must have heard someone moving. Llew and Morgan were with him. None of us dared budge. There was a commotion in the graveyard, and a dreadful scream. I looked out of the window, but it was dark, and I couldn't see anything. Then suddenly things went quiet. Ivan came back in by himself, the other two went off in the van, we heard it starting. They did not get back till much later."

Olga went on treading water, and looked at the limestone cliffs: an all too familiar feeling of unease had crept over her. Of course, it must have been the scream that she and Olga had heard when they were reconnoitring. But Tanya hadn't quite finished.

"Next morning," she continued, "some of us went out and found blood on one of the gravestones. We think someone may have been beaten up. Or even murdered. The boys must have carted him off, if there was only one, that is, we don't know."

"Oh, my God!" said Olga. "Murder? But you can't be sure, can you?"

"It was definitely a human scream," said Tanya.

Olga thought for a moment: best not to tell Tanya that she and Trevor had actually been there. It would only complicate things further.

"Well," she said, in as comforting a voice as she could manage. "You weren't mixed up in it yourself, were you? It's no concern of yours."

"We just don't know what's going to happen next," said Tanya, sobbing incongruously while she kept herself afloat. "Some of us want to run away, but we're back to the same old problems, being here illegally, not knowing

Chapter Six **173**

the language very well, with nowhere to go. And no marriages in sight. We're terrified that Ivan will start drug-running. We know he wants to."

Tanya was obviously hoping for some kind of help – from any quarter.

"I can't see how we can help you," said Olga, reading her thoughts. "But if I think of anything, I'll let you know. Thanks for telling me what you did, though. The picture is a bit clearer around Ivan. Mind, we're not in paradise either. We've got visa problems and we're short of cash."

"Oh," Tanya exclaimed, suddenly. "There is Ivan, he's coming in for a swim after all. I'd better get back to the others."

Olga turned and began to swim towards the other girls: yet another bit of unwelcome news to be passed on to Trevor. Was there no end in sight?

Trevor looked up as Olga plodded over the sand. She was obviously tense and dejected.

"I was just talking to Tanya Popova," she explained. "They're all as scared as ever. One new thing she told me, though. You remember that dreadful scream as we were leaving the graveyard? There must have been someone else prowling around, someone we didn't see. Anyway, Tanya said that shortly before the scream Ivan jumped up, as though he had heard something outside, and he rushed out with Llew and Morgan. The scream came shortly after they had gone. Then Llew and Morgan drove off in the van, and didn't come back for an hour or more. The next morning the girls found blood on one of the gravestones."

"Oh, my God!" exclaimed Trevor. "I wonder what he was up to?"

174   *Mother Russia*

"Trevor," said Olga, "I'm frightened again, there seems to be no end to it."

"Don't say anything to Masha or Dasha, though. They'll panic."

They sat in silence for a few moments, at a loss for words. Trevor put his arm around Olga's wet shoulders, it was the first time he had ever really embraced her. At moments like this – it was not the first – she gave the impression of an honest, rather frightened, woman who needed protection. She looked at him with a glint of a tear in her eye, but remained silent.

"Well, *we* haven't done anything wrong," he said. "We've talked about this before. It's true that we've seen Ivan a few times, and we've got his fridge, but that's as far as it has gone."

"Where are Masha and Dasha?" asked Olga, wanting to change the subject.

"They've gone to drink beer with Llew and Morgan. I wonder what time it is?" He looked at his watch. "Perhaps the *Evening Post* is out with the sewer story. I wonder whether they've found out any more about the bodies? I imagine it's on sale at the booth."

"Well," said Olga, "go over and see if you can get one. Perhaps they mention you. You'll be famous. Send Masha and Dasha back, if you see them."

On reaching the booth Trevor found that Dasha and Masha were indeed seated at one of the little tables in front of it, engrossed in beery conversation with their new-found friends. Clearly, they were not to be disturbed. But copies of the *Evening Post* were already stacked on the newspaper stand. Trevor bought one and checked at the headlines: the two-corpse episode was certainly on the front page. He made his way back to Olga, so that

Chapter Six   **175**

they could read it together. She looked at him expectantly.

"Olga, look at this! The whole page! 'Dismembered bodies...'

"Read it to me slowly," said Olga. "There may be words I don't understand."

Trevor read the following text:

The Evening Post

DISMEMBERED BODIES FOUND IN PENCLAWDD SEWER

By Gloria Evans

Life in Penclawdd was almost brought to a stop late yesterday afternoon by the startling discovery of two dismembered bodies in bags in the main sewer. In both cases the heads were missing. The main street was closed for an hour while the gruesome remains were retrieved, bagged, and dispatched to Llanelly mortuary. *The Evening Post* has elucidated that an experienced mortuary attendant was taken ill at the sight of them, and himself required medical attention.

The various organs, incongruously lodged in the town's main outlet, belonged to an apparently middle-aged man and a woman in her thirties. The police, with the help of a credit card, were able to identify the male body as that of Mr. Emlyn Davies, a social worker from Tredigar, unmarried and living alone. His relatives have been informed.

"Emlyn Davies!" cried Olga, "Emlyn Davies!"

"You knew him?" said Trevor in astonishment.

"Yes! But go on, I'll tell you in a minute."

The woman's body has not yet been identified but a red shoe left on one of the feet carried a Russian label, and there was a Russian coin in one of her pockets. Evidently, she came from that distant land.

The retrieval operation was directed by Mr. Frank Parker, an . experienced sewerman, helped by Mr. Trevor Jenkins, who worked there earlier. 'It was a nasty business getting them out,' Mr. Parker told our reporter. 'Whoever put the bodies down there must have realised there would be a blockage that would cause problems for the whole community. They could at least have disposed of them in a more considerate and intelligent fashion. Regardless of intent, we all have a civic duty to respect our sewers.'

Yesterday, the local police held a press conference to appeal to the public for information.

'We have very few leads so far,' declared Superintendent Paul Watkins, who is in charge of the case. 'The heads are still missing. The cause of death has not been ascertained, but we are treating it as a double murder, of course – bodies don't get cut up like that by accident. A full scale investigation has been launched, and we will be interviewing people who knew Mr. Evans. He had no close relatives and lived alone. He had no police or criminal record. We have information to the effect that he was seen the night before in the fish and chip shop near Caersalem Chapel, Penclawdd, but after purchasing a portion of cod and a double helping of chips, he was lost sight of.'

In the absence of a head, the woman's torso will be difficult, if not impossible, to identify. Forensic experts say that she died two or three days earlier. She may have been Russian: if she had no relatives or friends here, and if she were an illegal immigrant, informants might not come forward.

Superintendent Watkins has asked anyone who can assist to telephone the special line, 999999.

The police say a photograph of Mr. Davies should soon be available for the public. They are most anxious to interview anyone who saw Mr. Davies after he left the fish and chip shop, or can give any information about him or his movements shortly be-fore he died. The bodies may have been dropped through a manhole in the vicinity of the chapel.

LOCAL REACTIONS

People living nearby were alerted to the problem when a nasty stench was detected around the manhole, due to a back-up of sewage. Mrs. Florry Thomas of 7 Mansel Street, who has lived just opposite the manhole for forty-three years, was the first to notice it. 'I was cleaning the front windows', she said. 'Normally, my husband Charlie does it, but he's down with his asthma at the moment, and I don't want him exerting himself. The smell was so bad, I knew something was wrong.

That manhole was very ill-fitting. I often thought you could trip up over it. And I think I saw a rat coming out once. Mind, I've always been suspicious of the sanitation in Penclawdd, it's a very low-lying place, and I don't think the council keeps it up proper.'

Mrs. Thomas telephoned the Water Board, who sent an officer of environmental health along, and a competent sewer team was quickly summoned. The police closed the road so that the workmen could operate properly. The traffic gets busy at that time in the afternoon, and the jam was considerable. There were unpleasant consequences for many local people, as Mrs. Thomas told us.

'I think the smell made Charlie's chest much worse,' she said, caringly. 'He had a terrible bout of coughing. The council ought to be better organised to deal with emergencies like this.'"

"That's all," said Trevor.

"And enough, too."

"So who was Emlyn Davies?"

178   *Mother Russia*

"If it was the same man, he came for a massage. And he was looking for Anna. I'm sure it must be her body. He knew she was living in Penclawdd, and he suspected that something funny was going on down there."

"Well, there it is," said Trevor. "It all fits together, doesn't it? Ivan kept Anna's body in the fridge until the fire, when he thought the kitchen might be inspected. So he got Llew and Morgan to shift it and hide it elsewhere, God knows where. That scream we heard in the cemetery must have been Emlyn Davies being murdered. I wonder why they did it, though?"

"He must have gone to the chapel to try and find out about Anna, without being seen. Just like us. But Ivan caught him, and murdered him. Good job he didn't catch us."

Trevor nodded in agreement.

"Ivan must have got desperate, with two bodies to dispose of. So after a day or two, the stupid fellow dumped them both in the sewer. Perhaps he panicked. Anna must have been dead for several days."

"Stupid," Olga agreed. "You can't just drop bodies into sewers. They don't do that, even in Russia."

"We might be the only persons who can connect the two corpses," Trevor continued. "Especially as they haven't got heads."

Olga grasped his hand and looked earnestly into his face; the world around Trevor receded, and he suddenly felt a warmth which until then had been all but absent from their relationship. He had always regarded Olga as rather a tough creature, underneath her sexy, if somewhat overripe exterior, a woman who could handle everything without male support, at least in the business sphere. But the recent events were transforming her into something

Chapter Six **179**

of a maiden in distress. He squeezed her hand. He reflected for a moment how things would be without her, and realised for the first time that her absence would leave a gap in his life. He had got used to seeing her every day: the fact that she was a little older than he suddenly didn't seem to matter.

"Don't worry, Olga. We still haven't done anything wrong. There's only the problem of your visa and your aunties'. That's no great shakes."

"It is if I get sent back to Russia," said Olga. "Things have got worse and worse. When we started, it was only the visas, well, the visas and the restaurant business. Then there was Ivan and his cockles and caviar, and his fridge, and his razor, then Anna's disappearance, the icons, and the Russian girls in Penclawdd. And now it's two murders. What shall we do?"

"What, indeed?" reflected Trevor. There was no doubt that the situation had deteriorated drastically. The moment had come for a difficult decision.

"It's a nightmare," he said. "But now that this has happened, we've simply got to tell the police. We are in possession of information which could help them. And if we don't come out with it, we may eventually be in trouble ourselves, even implicated. In a few days they'll have found out everything about Emlyn's movements, and quite possibly that he came to you for a massage. He may have told friends."

"We could always pretend that he didn't, or that we didn't know he was dead," said Olga. "That we hadn't seen the papers. I don't want to be questioned about anything."

"Well, your aunties may have seen him as well, and they could spill the beans, if only unintentionally. There aren't many people in Salubrious Passage, but outsiders may also have seen him go in. Anyway, in this country you're

180 *Mother Russia*

supposed to help the police. If we don't go to them ourselves they may think we are trying to hide something, and then they could get really nasty."

"And do what?"

"Detain us for questioning, deport you and Masha and Dasha, or whatever. If we help them, it may be a plus. No, now that Emlyn has been murdered, we've got to tell them all we know."

"But what about Ivan? If he finds out that we're helping the authorities he'll be along again with..." – she swallowed hard – "...his razor, and Llew and Morgan. And if the police find out about the girls they'll all be in prison... Oh, Trevor!" She could no longer withhold her tears.

"We'll have to risk it," said Trevor, firmly. "Ivan needn't know that we have gone to the police."

The discussion had got no further when Masha and Dasha reappeared, a little flushed after the beer.

"What's this?" Masha asked Olga. "Have you been crying? Has horrible Trevor said something nasty?"

"No, no," said Olga. "We're just having a little discussion about the business."

"That's enough to make anyone cry," said Masha.

"Things would be different if we were all happily married," said Dasha.

"We've got to go to the police about the report in today's paper," said Trevor.

"What report?" said Masha.

"This!" Trevor waved the sheet in front of her. "One of the two chopped-up bodies I told you about belonged to a man who came to Olga for a massage, and the other was almost certainly poor Anna's. We may be the only people who knew about both of them. The only thing is, the police haven't found the heads yet. They may be lying in the Loughor Estuary. Or hidden somewhere else."

"I don't want to go to the police," said Masha, filled with alarm.

"The police?" repeated her sister. "What about those two lovely boys? Will they be caught up in it as well?"

Trevor thought it best to leave the question unanswered, and began to gather the picnic things together. It was clear that nobody wanted to stay on the beach any longer.

"I'll ring the police station this evening," he said. "Let's get back to the car."

From Inspector Watkins's point of view, the surreptitious game of draughts was not going too well. Usually he enjoyed playing with Constable Moss – that is, during quiet moments in the office – but the murder case now on his hands tended to take up any spare moments. He looked impatiently at the chequered board in front of him: his lean features, cropped hair, and gold-rimmed spectacles gave him an ascetic, almost monkish, appearance. But as the reader of these lines will soon appreciate, he was a policeman to the core - inquisitive, meticulous in observing regulations, and anxious for promotion. He wondered when Constable Moss would return with the tea, another important part of his daily routine. There must be a queue down in the canteen, he thought; today they had left it a bit late.

He peered again at the disposition of draughtsmen and came to the conclusion that if Moss did not cotton on to

182   *Mother Russia*

his crafty intentions he, the inspector, might still win the game. It was, of course, all strictly against regulations (like the regular office sweepstakes), so the Inspector had instructed Policewoman Dobbs, his office assistant, not to disturb them. They were, he had told her, considering the dismembered bodies case, and needed to concentrate. The Inspector consoled himself with the thought that a good game of drafts sharpens the wit, to the benefit of the service, and, strange though it might seem, he had got a number of new insights into difficult cases while playing them. And if interrupted he could quickly conceal the board under the staff duty sheet, which was just about the right size.

"Emlyn Davies..," he mused. "Pity the murdered man had such a common name." Since the story had appeared in the *Evening Post* three Emlyn Davieses had been reported missing. One had left his wife for an unknown destination in 1968, and if the corpse were his, it would have to be eighty-seven years old. The man's wife, however, had not lost interest. The second Emlyn Davies had been working in a bank and absconded with several thousand pounds. Investigation had revealed that he was living with a new wife and three kids outside Buenos Aires. Another apparent sighting had come from a man and woman who ran a Russian restaurant in Salubrious Passage: they were supposed to be coming for questioning at five o'clock. If the female corpse was Russian, which was likely, given the shoe and the coins in the pocket, it was quite possible that she had gone to the only Russian establishment in Swansea.

Inspector Watkins looked at the clock: it was just a quarter to five. If Moss reappeared quickly, they could finish their game before the interview... His mind returned to the case.

Chapter Six **183**

... The Russian restaurant in Salubrious Passage... He had enquired at Swansea Guildhall and found that it had recently been shut down because there had been a fire and the kitchen was the source of food poisonings which had filled half a ward in Swansea Hospital. And if this Emlyn Davies went there, did he have a connection with Russia as well? Suddenly the inspector's right eye flickered, which it often did when he had a brilliant idea. The quirk had been noted and was something of a joke in the office.

"Russians," he thought. "Espionage, murdering people who perhaps knew too much? The Soviet Union had gone, but the espionage game was still very much alive. If so, what were they spying on in Penclawdd? *Is* there anything to spy on in Penclawdd?"

At that moment the door opened, and Sergeant Moss appeared with two plastic cups. Sergeant Moss was one of those people whose appearance is average in all respects and scarcely deserves comment.

"There was a crowd down there, was there?" said the Inspector.

"Not half," said Moss. "I thought I'd never get served. You said two sugars, didn't you?"

"I was just thinking about our murders, Constable," said the Inspector weightily, "No connection between them on the surface, it would seem, apart from sharing the same sewer. And yet in fact there may well be..."

The Constable looked at him intently.

"If the female corpse belonged to a Russian, as seems likely, that would explain why no one has come forward to report a woman missing. Either no one knew her, or she was living in Wales illegally! Or..." – he paused dramatically – "she was on a spying mission."

184   *Mother Russia*

"My God!" said Moss, catching his breath. "But what can you spy on in Penclawdd? The cocklebeds?" He gave a laugh, but noting his chief's displeasure, choked it quickly.

"There's nothing funny about it," said the Inspector. "There may well be an intelligence dimension – some secret installations we don't know about, even under the sands of the estuary. Electronic eyes, ears, monitoring equipment, God knows what. MI5 and MI6, and all the rest of it. There's a Russian woman and her boyfriend coming at five, they ran a Russian restaurant in Salubrious Passage, though it's closed now. Evidently they have something to tell us."

"I went there once," said Constable Moss. He was deeply impressed by his superior's perspicacity, but had not forgotten their game, either.

"Will we have time to finish this before she comes?" he asked.

"We can try. We've got a few minutes."

Both men sat down at the board, but the game was not destined to be finished at that point in time. No sooner had they recommenced than there was a tap on the door. The Inspector whipped the staff duty sheet over the board, as usual, and called out: "Come in!"

It was Policewoman Dobbs.

"Mr. Trevor Jenkins and Miss Olga Morozova have arrived, Inspector." she announced. "They're at the reception desk."

"They're a bit early," the Inspector snapped. "But no matter, show them up. Moss," he added, the moment the policewoman went off, "put the draught board in the bottom of the filing cabinet, will you. Try not to shift the pieces. We don't want to spoil the game."

Chapter Six **185**

A few minutes later the office door opened again, and Policewoman Dobbs ushered the visitors in. Trevor was in his old mac, but Olga had donned a gaudy yellow coat and her massage turban, which gave her a distinctly exotic air. Somehow she had thought it might make the police more sympathetic. Both she and Trevor were obviously nervous.

"Good afternoon," said the Inspector, with the polite but steely intonation that the police love to use in their dealings with the defenceless and innocent. "I'm Inspector Paul Watkins, and this is my colleague Constable Moss, we're working on the sewer case together. Thank you for offering to come. We prefer to have visitors here, rather than send officers around to people's houses. The neighbours talk, you know, and folk don't like it."

"We quite understand," said Trevor.

"We would like to ask you a few questions."

Trevor cleared his throat in anticipation.

"Now, you know there were two murders. I gather you might have some information on a certain Mr. Emlyn Davies, parts of whom were recently discovered in Penclawdd. We haven't found his head yet, it may have been washed out to sea, but we have obtained a photo of him from his workplace. Please look at this. He was of medium height, probably in his thirties, and spoke Welsh."

"How do you know he spoke Welsh," said Trevor in astonishment.

"There was a scrap of Welsh newspaper in his shirt pocket."

"Yes," said Olga, examining the photograph. "That's him. He came for a massage. He was a social worker."

186   *Mother Russia*

"Excellent," said the Inspector, rubbing his hands. "Now we have some indirect confirmation of the identity of the corpse. But I thought you ran a restaurant," he added.

"I've been doing some massaging work while it's closed," said Olga. "I have a few clients who come in. We've got to keep going somehow."

"Where do you do it?"

"Wherever they want it," said Olga. "Shoulders, back, hips... Some of the men wanted..."

"I don't mean that," the Inspector interrupted her hastily. "Where is your massage parlour?"

"In Salubrious Passage."

"On the restaurant premises, in effect?"

"Yes, we put extra curtains up. There was nothing to stop us using it for other purposes, provided we did not serve food."

"I'm not sure about that," Constable Moss cut in. "Massage parlours have to be licensed, too. Do you have any physiological certificates?"

"No," said Olga, "only my two cooking diplomas. They've got gold lettering on them."

"All right," said the Constable. "That's not relevant. We're not interested in cookery, with gold letters or not."

"The lady is trying to assist the police in the performance of their duties, Constable," said the Inspector gently. "I imagine any unregistered activity was inadvertent and short-lived."

"Oh, the massage business only lasted a few days," said Trevor. "Takings were nominal, and you'll be declaring them for tax, won't you, Olga."

She nodded in assent.

Chapter Six **187**

"Well, let's get back to this unfortunate victim," said the Inspector. "When did he come to see you?"

"About a week ago."

"And you massaged him in the usual manner."

"Yes," said Olga. "Back and shoulders, mostly."

"Now, did he say anything which you might have regarded as unusual or suspicious?"

"Only one thing," said Olga. "He said he was a social worker, helping women in distress. And he taught them something called therapeutic Welsh. He wanted to know, like you, whether I knew any Russians. In fact, I think that's really why he came for a massage. The body contact was not the main thing."

"Was he looking for anyone in particular?"

"Yes," said Olga. "There was a Russian girl called Anna. He said she had disappeared from his classes. He thought it was very unusual, and he was worried about her. He said if the numbers went down the local council might close the class."

The two policemen looked at one another, enjoying another moment of profound satisfaction. Thanks to their perceptive questioning, the investigation had moved forward. They had discovered a possible, nay probable, link between the bodies: Emlyn Davies may have been looking for the dead woman, who was Russian, and her name was Anna. But what lay behind that? Both officers suppressed any visible reaction, because the public were not supposed to be privy to police thought. But with better prospects for promotion, their mood improved noticeably.

"Did you ever see or meet this Anna?" said the Inspector.

188   *Mother Russia*

Trevor and Olga exchanged an almost imperceptible glance. The same idea flashed through both of their minds: should they tell the police about Ivan Kravchenko's fridge and what came out of it? The answer to that question, thought Trevor, must be no. Truthfully. Neither of them had either seen or met a living Anna, and the rest was supposition, or almost so.

"She never came to us for a meal," said Trevor. "And neither of us ever met her."

"Did Emlyn Davies tell you anything about her?"

"Well, he said he hadn't seen her for some time, and he was afraid she might have got mixed up with undesirables."

"Undesirables? Do you have any idea whom he meant?"

That was a question, thought Trevor, which might be usefully answered. This might be a way of getting rid of Ivan and his lousy fridge altogether. If the police got onto him, he might go.

"No one specific," he said, "but we've had a few tough customers in Mother Russia. One of them was a Russian called Ivan Kravchenko. It's possible that he knew her. He came to the restaurant a few times, and offered us a business deal."

"What was that?"

"Selling caviar and sturgeon from Russia, through his so-called cockle business. He claimed he was keeping supplies in his own fridge in our kitchen. We didn't want to have anything to do with it. It was a hopeless proposal. Caviar and sturgeon are too expensive for any of our customers. And the fridge took up a lot of space. But he turned nasty and insisted on us keeping it. We thought perhaps there was something illegal behind it, but we had no proof, and it was no business of ours, anyway. If you're

Chapter Six **189**

running a restaurant, you have to deal with your customers as they come. Otherwise you lose them."

Inspector Watkins positively glowed with interest.

"A business associate. Do you have his surname or address? What did he look like?"

"He's called Ivan Kravchenko, but we don't have an address. He's a big man, with a broad, Slav face, grey hair, blue eyes, obviously tough, in his early fifties. He usually dressed in a smart suit," said Olga.

"Get the Neath crowd photos out, will you?" the Inspector ordered Constable Moss.

The good Constable went to a filing cabinet in the corner of the room and after a certain amount of shuffling produced a battered green folder.

"That's not it," said the Inspector testily. "That's Will Higgins, we did him for sexually molesting a horse."

"A horse?" asked Trevor.

"A Shire filly called Doris," replied the Inspector with a grimace. "A revolting case. But not one to be discussed with the public."

"Well, they should have cleared the file away," Constable Moss went on rummaging. "I think the Neath file has gone up to Cardiff for archiving. And Florry cleared a lot of stuff out last week."

"Well, she shouldn't have cleared that, it's not finished yet."

"Here it is," said the Constable at last, with a note of triumph in his voice. "Disorders in Neath. Misfiled a bit though, in with the soliciting and other misdemeanour charges. There was a rash of cases behind Swansea market, wasn't there, involving two sex-starved Nigerian

190   *Mother Russia*

bus drivers. Remember, we sent Florry down in civvies, and she managed to get herself propositioned. She arrested both of them on the spot."

"Sex, sex, sex," said the Inspector impatiently. "It's sickening. Cata-bloody-strophic. That's the nice thing about the Penclawdd sewers case, no sexual dimension."

"Well, we don't know, do we?" said the Constable. "Perhaps ..."

"It's clearly murder," the Inspector interrupted him tensely, "not merely a few gropes. Let me see the papers."

He thumbed through the file and pulled out a photograph. "Was this the man?" he said, turning to his visitors.

Trevor and Olga peered at an indistinct photograph of a man entering what looked like a supermarket. Despite the blurring, there was no doubt about his identity.

"Yes, that's Ivan," said Trevor. "A nasty bit of work, if I may say so. Olga's quite afraid of him. Why you are interested in him?"

"Kravchenko was one of several Russians involved in a nasty brawl in Neath a few weeks ago. It was reported in the press. But why were you suspicious of him yourselves?"

"When we came to think about it, it all seemed a bit over the top... the cockle business, caviar and sturgeon from Russia, the fridge that he always kept locked. And he said that we might need protection against criminals from Neath. We were afraid he was running a protection racket."

"When he first came to the restaurant he forgot his briefcase with a razor in it," Olga added. "There was dried blood on the blade. He came and picked it up next day."

Chapter Six **191**

"You didn't report it to the police?"

"Well, it was none of our business," said Olga. "We only looked in the briefcase by chance. How were we to know there was anything wrong?"

"Perhaps he was a careless barber," Trevor repeated a witticism he had made earlier, "or cut himself when he was shaving. We saw him a bit drunk and unsteady."

"So he said he kept the caviar and sturgeon locked in the fridge," said the Inspector, moving on. "But do you need a whole fridge for caviar? And a big one at that? That's a bit strange, isn't it? What else did he keep in it?"

"We never saw it open. Caviar is valuable stuff, of course."

"Didn't he give you a key?"

"No," said Trevor. "He let us have a few pots of the stuff for our own fridge, to cover any customers' orders. But there were none." Trevor wondered for a moment whether he should bring up the topic of icons, though it sounded absurd. On the other hand, why not?

"One of Olga's aunties saw a stack of icons in it as well. She happened to be in the kitchen one day when he opened it."

"Icons," said Constable Moss. "Does this Ivan deal in icons as well? Russian antiques! They might be stolen, or imported illegally!"

"I don't know," said Trevor. "I don't think they're very old, in fact he gets them painted here. They're not standard icons, they're sort of..." – he paused – "funny, and I think the Russian Church has objections to them. Some priests came to complain about them, in fact."

"Dismembered bodies and razors," said the Inspector, "caviar and icons! My God, what a case!"

192   *Mother Russia*

"Confusing, isn't it?" remarked Constable Moss.

"We'll have to look at the fridge as well," said the Inspector in an authoritative tone of voice. "It may be perfectly legal, but things are not always what they seem. The reactions of the Russian Church are of no concern to us, but they might have lighted upon some illegality."

He paused dramatically.

"Given what we know about him already, this Ivan must be a prime suspect. The next thing is to get hold of him for questioning, but we don't know where he lives. Our best chance of picking him up is when he next comes to Mother Russia. We can get him to open the fridge with the police as witnesses."

"What about the chapel?" thought Trevor. "But if the police go there, they'll find the girls. Better let them come to Mother Russia, and not mention the chapel at all. We've got nothing to hide at the restaurant."

"Oh," said Olga, anxiously, "Mr. Inspector, we've had so much trouble recently. If Ivan finds out that we are helping you he'll be furious. And he's got men helping him as well. They'll attack us. Couldn't you catch him some other way? Or inspect the fridge when they are not there."

"I'm not sure we have sufficient evidence to break into it," said the Inspector. "There are limits to police powers, you know." He puffed his breast, to indicate that they were not too numerous. "And as members of the public you have a civic duty to assist the police in the performance of their duties."

"We're not under a civic duty to expose ourselves to thugs," said Trevor.

There was an awkward silence, and the Inspector cleared his throat, changing gear, as it were.

Chapter Six **193**

"I gather you are a Russian national, madam," he said, looking at Olga.

"So that's what he's going for," thought Trevor.

"Yes," said Olga, trying not to sound apprehensive.

"I'd like you to bring your passport in tomorrow. What visa have you got? When does it expire? Are any other members of your family with you? Do you have a work permit?"

Trevor decided that they did not have a chance.

"As a matter of fact," he said aloud, "Olga's visa is perfectly valid, but it expires in two weeks-time. She fully expects to get it extended. She has two aunts here, they're all in the same position."

"Well," said the inspector in icy tones, "extension is by no means automatic, you know. We'll have to have a word with the Home Office about that. The residence permit might be extended, and it might not... Of course, if Madam Morozova were voluntarily helping the police on a difficult case, we might be able to put in a good word. Otherwise, we might even object. We'll have to see how things turn out."

"The old bugger has won," thought Trevor. "Of course, we'd rather have the police as friends rather than enemies," he said. "We will help if we can. What would you expect us to do?"

"Very little," said the Inspector. "We just want admission to your premises when you next expect Ivan, so that we can detain him for questioning. With any of his associates, if they come. We haven't got any hard evidence of his involvement in the murders yet, but things might move in that direction. So it's a question of you letting us know when you expect him. We'll detain him and make him open the fridge on the spot. Our files on the Neath business are still open."

"He said he was coming tomorrow evening," said Olga. "He usually comes round six."

"Okay," said Inspector Watkins. "I'll be there personally with some officers in plain clothes, well in advance. It'll be as though we are all coming for a massage. We'll hide on your premises and confront the gentleman at an appropriate moment. You have nothing at all to fear. Leave your telephone number with us, please, so that we can contact you if necessary. Incidentally, we'll have to have your phone tapped, so as to monitor any calls from him. I think that's all. I'm glad we've been able to sort things out," he concluded hurriedly, before they could change their minds and complicate things. "Show the lady and gentleman out, will you, Constable?"

Out in the street, Trevor and Olga looked at one another and paused for breath. Things had moved much faster than they had anticipated: and now they had a police ambush to contend with.

"When will it all end?" thought Olga for the umpteenth time.

Chapter Seven

(Another chapel visit: two elderly spinsters spring their trap, and more astonishing events occur at 'Mother Russia'.)

"Here we are, back again," said Trevor. "Keep your head down. The van's still here, so they can't have gone yet. We'll have to chance our luck."

Olga and he were once again crouching behind one of the gravestones in Penclawdd Chapel cemetery, though this time they had a bright, cloudless sky above them, such as they had enjoyed during their afternoon at Caswell. After getting back from the cop-shop the evening before, they had held yet another council of war and told the old aunts about forthcoming events, so that they should not spoil anything. They had also decided that with the ambush looming they should try and warn Tanya and the girls. Nothing could, of course, be divulged about police activities: but obviously the girls should be told that Ivan was in deep trouble and be warned that it would be wise for them to keep themselves out of the picture. Otherwise they might be caught up in a police investigation which could cause them nothing but trouble.

"Why should they go anywhere?" Olga asked.

"Oh, it'll be the lunch-time boozing session," Trevor answered, "just the three men, I hope. That's what I'm counting on, anyway. We may just be able to contact the girls while they've gone off. If the police are coming this afternoon we haven't got that much time."

Trevor pulled out a handkerchief and wiped his neck, while Olga helped with little pats.

196   *Mother Russia*

"My God, it's hot," he said.

"It gets much hotter than this on the Volga!"

"Continental climate," said Trevor. "Short, hot summers and very cold winters." He cast another cautious glance at the chapel entrance.

"I hope they go off soon," he repeated. "We can't wait too long."

"Oh," said Olga, suddenly. "There's an ant crawling up my leg. I think we're on a nest."

"Well, wipe it off," said Trevor a little impatiently. "We can't worry about ants just now. Let's find another gravestone. Come on."

They crept to a piece of masonry which seemed to be ant-free, but still allowed them to keep Ivan's van in view. An old tabby cat was sunning himself on top of it.

"Oh, look," said Trevor.   He liked felines. "It's the cemetery cat!"

"It must live here," said Olga. "Perhaps it likes the atmosphere."

"Or the mice."

"It must have witnessed quite a few passings," said Olga.

Suddenly a stone flew through the air, narrowly missing the animal, but causing it to look up in alarm. A second stone followed, prompting it to jump off the gravestone and disappear. A shrill boyish laugh broke out.

The interlopers looked in the direction from which the missile had come. A couple of dishevelled urchins, one ginger-haired, one dark and wearing bent glasses, were ensconced behind another grave, watching them. The

Chapter Seven **197**

ginger-haired boy made an unmistakably rude gesture with two fingers.

"Those damn' kids," said Trevor angrily. "They'll give us away, and ruin everything."

"They think we're going to do something adult," said Olga. "And want to watch."

"Here?" said Trevor. "In broad daylight?"

He rose a little, and gestured towards the offending pair.

"Go away, will you," he said in a loud whisper.

"Go away your bloody self," said the boy in bent glasses.

"*Up iw!*" said the other.

"That's the local schools for you," said Trevor.

At that moment, perhaps as a gesture of bravado, the ginger-haired one threw another stone towards the spot whither the cat had disappeared. He aimed much too high, however, and the stone crashed straight through one of the chapel windows, with a tinkle of broken glass. The boys fled instantly, just before the chapel door opened and Ivan emerged, followed shortly by Llew and Morgan.

"Keep down," hissed Trevor. "They'll see us if we try and get away now."

There was the sound of scrambling and a couple of thumps as the boys, agile as monkeys, climbed over the wall and dropped out of sight.

"I think it's only kids!" Ivan's voice carried well through the quiet afternoon air. "Perhaps they've run off."

Trevor and Olga could see some of Ivan's girls coming out into the chapel porch to see what was going on. He gestured them back inside.

198   *Mother Russia*

"Okay, boys," he said, turning to his companions. "We'll have a look around anyway... If we catch any of the little bastards we'll teach them a lesson. Let's split up three ways. You do one side each, and I'll do the middle."

Ivan turned and made his way cautiously between the rows of gravestones nearest to him, the path leading, as it happened, directly to Trevor and Olga's hiding place. They could just hear the swish of his trousers in the weeds and long grass, and crouched lower in dreadful anticipation of discovery. The man was capable of anything. Trevor had a recollection of the dangerous moment he had experienced in Salubrious Passage, with the very same actors. But now he could feel Olga trembling with fear beside him. Ivan's rather stylish leather shoes, with bits of wet leaf and clay on them, came into view. One more step and ... Suddenly, there was a diversion, tiny but significant.

"Oh," cried Morgan from the other side of the cemetery. "There's an old cat! I bet that's what they were aiming at!"

Ivan advanced no further.

"They've gone, anyway," he said. "They probably jumped over the wall. And I'm getting my shoes dirty..." He turned and began to swish his way back. "We'd better be off to the pub. We'll have to get some glass for the window."

"A bit of cardboard would do," said Llew. Trevor and Olga looked at one another, sharing an expression of profound relief.

"Jesus!" said Trevor, waving his hand in front of his face, fan-wise. "That was close."

"Oh, Trevor!" said Olga. "You were wonderful, so calm and collected!"

Chapter Seven **199**

"No, I wasn't," he replied. "To tell you the truth, they frightened the shit out of me."

Llew and Morgan were standing by the van, while Ivan ventured into the chapel alone. He returned a few minutes later with a couple of bags. One or two of the girls came out into the porch to see them depart.

"We'll be back in a couple of hours," said Ivan, again loud enough for Trevor and Olga to hear. "Same as usual this evening!"

And with that the three men climbed into the van and drove off.

"Well, we mustn't waste any time," said Trevor. "We'd better get in and have a word with them straight away."

"Better wait for a few minutes," said Olga, restraining him. "In case the men have forgotten something and come back."

They sat there for five minutes more: had it not been for the tense circumstances, it would have been a pleasant interlude. An old mulberry tree cast a shimmering shadow over their new hiding place, so the sun troubled them less. There was the whisper of a breeze off the Loughor estuary and the hum of insects: the murmur of the town scarcely reached them, hardly more than the sound of a vehicle revving, a horn, perhaps, a dog barking. Olga rested her head gently against her hand, which she had laid on the mossy stone, and closed her eyes. Trevor looked at her. It was the first time he had seen her look so peaceful.

He thought of the extraordinary series of events which had occurred over the last few days, events which might possibly have changed his life in a completely unexpected manner. He and Olga had been thrown together quite a lot, something which he did not anticipate when he first made the Mother Russia deal. It just happened that he had the money and thought the restaurant might be a good investment. He looked at Olga again: yes, he had to admit it, he *was* getting more attached to her. She was intelligent, caring and very original, in the Swansea context at least. She always seemed to be coming out with interesting tales from her past. And if she was to be believed, she was only about a year older than he – no great shakes.

Then, quite unexpectedly, she opened her eyes. It was as though she knew he was gazing at her.

"Do you love your little Olga, Trevushka?" she said, "just a little bit?"

"Come on," said Trevor, rising to his feet. "We'd better go and see the girls."

Rather than tap on the chapel door – which might have caused some alarm – they hurried to the window which they had used before.

"There's Tanya," said Olga.

Inside Trevor could see a group of girls. Olga tapped the glass, and some of them looked over. "She's recognised me," she said to Trevor. "They're going to let us in. I think they want us to go to a side entrance."

They went around the building, and indeed came upon a little door, which opened just as they reached it. Tanya was waiting for them inside.

"Come in!" She was clearly apprehensive.

Trevor and Olga found themselves in a narrow corridor, rather shabby and smelling of damp, just as might be expected in an old neglected building.

Chapter Seven **201**

"Olga," said Tanya. "Why have you come?"

"How long do you think they'll be away?" Olga countered.

"The men?" said Tanya. "An hour at least. They've gone boozing. You're safe for a bit. We'd hear the van. But why have you come?"

"To warn you that Ivan is in big trouble," said Trevor. "The police are after him. We are not allowed say anything about it, but we think you all ought to get the hell out of here. The police are bound to come nosing around."

"But we're not doing anything wrong! We're only trying to earn a living!"

"Have you got visas?"

Tanya was silent.

"So, you don't want to be picked up by the police, do you?" said Olga.

"I don't know what the others will say," said Tanya.

"I think the best thing for me to do it to have a quick word with them," said Olga.

"I'll get them into the chapel," said Tanya. "Go in and wait."

Trevor and Olga went into the small hall. It was a nonconformist chapel like any other: rather drab pews, a pulpit, tall windows, a wooden first-floor gallery and a harmonium in one corner. The smell of damp was apparent here, too. Olga looked around with some interest, and nodded to the girls who were already in there.

"Never been in a Methodist Chapel before, have you, Olg," Trevor asked.

202 *Mother Russia*

"No, only Russian Orthodox churches."

"I had to go every Sunday," said Trevor. "It was deadly boring. Put me off God for ever."

A few other girls began to filter in, some sat down in the pews, others stood in the aisles. No outsiders had ever come before, and there were expressions of surprise. "Who are they? What do they want?" Tanya went up into the pulpit, so that everyone could see her, while Trevor and Olga stood on the steps, a little lower.

"These are my friends Olga Morozova and Trevor Jenkins," Tanya declared. "They've come to give us an important message."

"Go on Olga, you tell them," said Trevor.

"Hello girls," said Olga. "As you can hear I am Russian. I've been living in Swansea for some months. Some of you may have seen me before, when you came to our restaurant, Mother Russia."

There were murmurs of recognition. The girls stared at her, intent on every word.

"Trevor and I have come here today to warn you about a possible police raid."

"I've never had a policeman," said someone. "Do they pay well?"

"Same as everybody else, I suppose," said another.

"No, seriously," Olga continued. "Ivan Ivanovich has been up to some pretty nasty tricks, and the police are after him. For instance, he was involved in a brawl, with a knife fight, up in Neath."

"That would be with the Ukrainian gang," said another girl. "There's a man called Fedor who is trying to muscle in on his business."

Chapter Seven **203**

"Apart from that," Olga continued, "there's poor Anna."

"Yes, Anna," said someone. "Where has she got to? None of us know. She just disappeared."

"Dead," said Olga, in a low voice.

The sense of shock in the chapel was palpable. Olga paused to let it sink in. "She wanted to break away and start a new life. She got into contact with a Welsh support group for girls in need. Ivan must have found out about it," Olga went on, "and he was afraid that she would blow his escort work. Or go over to the Ukrainians. So he killed her. Or had her killed."

"How do you know?"

"They've found a cut-up body, and it's almost certainly hers. It was in the paper last night. But we think that before he chopped it up, he was keeping it in a fridge in our restaurant. That is, until he could get rid of it."

Despite their robust calling, some of the ladies had a squeamish streak, and there were gasps of horror.

"Oh," said someone, "it'll be enough to finish her poor mother, when she hears about it."

"Where's the body now?" asked one of the girls, evidently of a more pious nature. "Is there enough of it left for an Orthodox burial? How much do you have to have, anyway?"

"There *could* be a funeral," said Olga. "Some Russian priests have been around the pubs looking for converts."

"They haven't found the head yet," said Trevor. "I would imagine that's the most important bit. But that's not all, either. It's almost certain that Ivan committed another murder. A man called Emlyn Davies, who knew Anna as well."

204   *Mother Russia*

"He came for a massage," Olga explained. "He was looking for anyone who might have known Anna. He was worried about her disappearance, and he was trying to help her. He may have found out something about Ivan's activities, and suspected that the caviar and the cockle business was a cover for something more sinister."

"I think Ivan wanted to go on to heroin and cocaine," said Tanya. "The Ukrainians are doing it already. Ivan hasn't started that yet, at least he never asked us, but it's getting more likely."

"We think Emlyn came snooping around here to find out more," said Olga. "It looks as though Ivan slipped out and killed him in the graveyard. Some of you may have heard him scream."

"That's right," said someone. "We did. But we were too scared to go out. There's some blood on a gravestone."

"And so," Trevor continued, "the police have two murder cases on their hands, apart from the prostitution and drug angles. And the illegal immigrants. It'll be big. The *Evening Post* is on to the murders already."

In the pews the expressions of horror gave way to animated discussions of what to do next.

"Well, that's the problem," said Tanya, as though voicing a common opinion. "We've got to get out of here before the police come. But where can we go?"

"Anywhere is safer for you than Penclawdd or Neath," said Olga. "But don't go yet, or Ivan Ivanovich will smell a rat. Then he'll be after US in Mother Russia, and the police will think we warned him on purpose. All I can say is, it's better to go off this evening, under cover of dark, as though you were going out on a normal round. *Please* don't do anything before. Leave your stuff here."

"We haven't got much," one of the girls called out.

Chapter Seven **205**

"We can come and collect it later, when it all quietens down. I think that's all we have to say," Olga concluded.

"And enough, too," said Tanya. "Girls, I think Olga has done us a big favour by warning us."

"Play it cool, girls," said Trevor. "If Ivan doesn't suspect anything he won't touch you. When he's inside, you'll have nothing to fear. You won't have visas, but you won't have Ivan to cope with, either. When he comes back, act normally, and go off to the bars as usual. Pack your things now, and don't show him."

"What about Llew and Morgan?" someone asked. "Are the police after them as well?"

"As far as we know," said Olga, "they haven't been involved in anything, except driving Ivan's van and carting a corpse or two around. But they might claim they did not know what they were carrying. They're more interested in beer than anything else."

"Don't worry about that pair," Trevor added. "I don't think they would touch you, anyway. There'd be no point. But now, I think we'd better be off, while the going's good."

The girls started a lively discussion amongst themselves: what should they do?

"By the way," Olga said to Tanya, as they were leaving the hall. "As if it matters, what's this lewd icon business?"

Tanya gave a wry smile.

"I'll show you," she said. "It'll only take a minute. It's a joke really, something for some of the girls to do in their spare time."

She pointed to a narrow stairway. The three of them climbed up and found themselves on a little landing. Then Tanya threw open a door to reveal a cramped room, perhaps a meeting room or classroom, which was being used as a workshop. A few easels stood around, with icons attached, and there was a strong smell of oil paint.

"Some of us have got quite good at it," said Tanya. "We have these tracings to start off with, and then we paint onto them. This is a nice one." She picked up a finished icon. "The Black Virgin of Verkhoyansk with an extra large bosom. And here's one of the squint-eyed Saint Vassilii of Pechorskaya Lavra, holding a candle in one hand and a large male member in the other."

"No wonder we had two priests along to complain," said Olga.

"Ivan has been selling them for us," said Tanya. "I imagine that he is making a lot of money out of it, but we don't get much."

"We'd better go," said Trevor. "They may come back early."

So off he and Olga went, leaving a great deal of consternation behind them. But they had, at least, done what they thought was right in the circumstances.

The red single-decker bus pulled up to the stop and the sliding doors opened. Nobody wanted to get off, but the driver assumed that the two angelic old ladies who were waiting at the kerbside would want to get on. They were evidently arguing about the number.

"Does this go past the Red Cow in Penclawdd?" one of them asked, with a heavy accent.

"Yes, dear," said the driver in the gentle tone he used for passengers who looked as though they might soon be boarding a hearse, horizontally.

Chapter Seven **207**

"Can you tell us where to get off, please?"

"Of course, love. Going to watch the billiard competition, are you?"

The two old ladies looked at each other with some surprise.

"Is there a competition? My sister's quite good at billiards," said Masha.

"It's the Gower stakes, beginning at three!"

"Oh, how interesting."

The doors closed and the vehicle pulled away. The new passengers observed the unfamiliar streets with interest. Eventually it stopped in front of a nondescript pub which, rather like Mother Russia, had formerly been two terraced houses. The two old ladies got off, thanking the driver as they did so.

"Bit old to be taking an interest in billiards," he thought. "But it takes all sorts to make a world."

Masha and Dasha stood on the pavement for a moment, looking at the pub.

"Well, here it is," said Dasha. "Let's go in."

She pulled a large, silver watch out of her pocket. "We've got a bit of time yet. They probably don't come until about one. The bank is open till five, though."

"I wonder whether there's anyone playing billiards yet," said Masha.

They pushed their way into the public bar, which was quite crowded.

"I hope they do turn up," said Masha. "It's a long way for us to come for nothing. You've got everything, have you?"

208   *Mother Russia*

Dasha responded by patting her abdomen, covered by a frilly white blouse, and then opening the top of her bag, so that her sister could catch sight of the bulky brown envelope inside.

"There's a table over there, by the window. If we sit there we can see everybody who comes in."

"Well, if they don't come, we can always watch the billiards," said Dasha. "I was in the Komsomol team, remember?"

"Those were the days!" said Masha. "What are we having to drink?"

"Get a couple of gin and tonics, the usual. I hope you've got enough money."

Masha edged her way through the crowd at the counter and when her turn came she gave her order. She got the drinks on a small tray and carried them back.

No sooner had they settled, however, than Dasha's gaze shifted to the large billiard table alongside the bar.

"The competition hasn't started yet, but some people are playing," she said.

A heavily-built man in an open-necked shirt and braces was chalking a cue. His game had evidently just finished, and it was apparent from his satisfied grin that he had won it.

"I'll just go and have a little look," said Dasha. She rose and went over to the green baize.

The man with the cue was clearly amused by her interest: it was not often that he had spectators of that age and sex.

"Like a game, grandma?" he asked jovially.

Chapter Seven **209**

"Yes," answered Dasha. "I learned to play many years ago in Russia."

"I take on all comers," said the man. "A fiver to the winner."

"All right," said Dasha, rolling up the sleeves of her blouse. "Put the balls out."

One or two of the drinkers gathered around to watch.

The man in braces started with a series of shots which allowed him to pocket several balls: he was clearly a skilled player. Indeed, a trace of embarrassment crossed his face – the old girl had offered to play him, but was it fair to take her money? She was probably on a tiny pension.

Dasha, however, was watching him with an experienced eye, holding her cue in the crux of her arm, like a knightly lance. At last her opponent missed a pocket, and her chance came. With consummate skill she pocketed several balls herself. At one point she needed to reach an awkward spot on the table, and her opponent offered her a long-handled cue support.

"Oh, I don't need that," she exclaimed, "a lot of people don't use them where I come from."

"Want me to lift you up, love? How will you manage?"

Ignoring his offer, Dasha flung herself onto the expanse of green, revealing a small area of red flannelette as she did so. The bystanders exchanged amused glances.

A satisfying click followed, and in no time at all she had got the last ball into a pocket. The man in braces leaned unsteadily on his cue, reached for his wallet, and sighed. Things hadn't gone at all as he anticipated.

"Would you like another game?" asked Dasha brightly, as she took the five pound note.

210   *Mother Russia*

"I don't think so," said he. "I'll treat myself to another pint instead."

A small round of applause went up among the onlookers, and Dasha looked around expectantly. Did anyone else want a game? No? She retired, reluctant but triumphant, to the table at the window.

"Mother never liked you playing billiards in Verkhoyansk," said Masha. "Ladies don't do it in Russia."

"It has its advantages, though, doesn't it?" her sister replied. "But look!" A tense note crept into her voice. "They're here!"

At that moment, who should walk in but Llew and Morgan: their gait leisurely, and their faces wreathed in smiles, doubtlessly in anticipation of ample lunch-time refreshment. At first they did not notice the two sisters.

"They don't know what's coming, do they?" Masha murmured.

"Good God!" said Llew, as he caught sight of them. "The old girls from Mother Russia. It looks as though they are following us around, don't it? How did they know we come here?"

"They asked us in Caswell," said Morgan. "Remember? But it doesn't matter."

"Perhaps they'll buy us a few drinks. As a matter of fact, I think they promised us. Let's go over."

"What a surprise," said Llew, when they reached the table. "Have you been here long?"

"Only a few minutes," said Dasha.

"Long enough to play a game of billiards," said Masha. "She just won five pounds. It'll pay for the drinks."

The two men perked up visibly.

Chapter Seven **211**

"What will you have?" Masha asked.

"A Bloody Mary," said Morgan. "Vodka for a special occasion."

"Same for me," said Llew. "Two Bloody Marys."

"Masha means Mary in Russian," said Masha, with a giggle. "Two Bloody Mashas, then." Dasha rose to get them.

"Don't forget to switch the bloody thing on," Masha told her sister in a tense whisper, as she left the table. Llew and Morgan were still laughing at their own joke.

"Are you hungry?" Masha asked the men as they waited. "Like a snack?"

"Not yet!" said Morgan.

"Hungry for love!" said Llew, and they laughed again.

"Where's Ivan?"

"He's gone up to Penarth to pick up some caviar, we think."

"And how are things going in the transport business?"

"Just the same," said Morgan. "No great shakes."

"Still delivering things," said Llew.

"Where?" asked Masha.

"Here and there," said Llew.

"What things?" said Dasha, returning with the drinks. She had caught the gist of what was being said.

"Oh, this and that," said Morgan.

The four of them laughed, somewhat childishly.

"Corpses, perhaps?" said Masha, suddenly dead serious.

212   *Mother Russia*

The men went on laughing for a second or two: that is, until they grasped the import of what she had said.

"What?" said Llew, in as incredulous a tone as he could muster. "Corpses? We don't know nothing about corpses."

Around the little table there was a stunned silence: by comparison, the noise at the bar seemed to get louder – raucous conversation, the clink of glasses, with the click of billiard balls in the background. The erstwhile mood of jollity had evaporated completely. Morgan paled.

"Look what you done to him," said Llew, in an attempt to change the topic of conversation. "He's a delicate lad, he don' like anything like that. He's all upset. Are you all right, Mog?"

"Well, he may be upset," said Dasha, "but we saw him carrying one. And you, the two of you together."

The men were obviously struggling to come to terms with the situation, their drinks untouched.

"No, we didn't carry no corpses," said Llew again. "All the stuff was packed in plastic bags, anyway."

"We didn't know what was in them," Morgan added helpfully. "We was told that a lot of it was caviar and them big sturgeon."

"And the sacks that were thrown down the drain?"

There was another silence.

"Dasha, show them," Masha commanded.

Dasha fumbled in her shopping bag for a moment, and pulled out a bulky envelope. She opened it carefully, turned it upside down, and indicated to Morgan that he should hold out his hands. Somewhat bewildered, he did so. A red slipper dropped into his outstretched palms.

"Have you seen that before?" asked Dasha.

Chapter Seven **213**

Morgan turned it over and pretended to examine it closely. His eyes watered a little, or so it seemed. He turned to Llew for guidance. There was a kind of hopelessness in his gaze.

"Er, no," he said.

"Llew?" said Masha. "Take it and have a good look. There's a label inside!"

Llew took the slipper and looked behind the heel. "Made in Moscow," he said. "No, I never saw it either."

Dasha carefully retrieved the slipper, and put it back in the envelope.

"Funny," said Dasha. "Because it fell off the corpse Ivan was keeping in his fridge. When you carried it out to the van."

"What fridge?" said Morgan.

"No we didn't," said Llew. "There wasn't no corpse in that fridge. Ha, ha! A corpse in a fridge!"

It didn't sound very convincing, and his mind, such as it was, was racing. "Had the old cows really seen them? If so, why hadn't they gone to the police? What could be done now? Bribe them? Do a frightener on them? Do them up? Do them in? But there were two of them, and pretty tough and wiry at that. It was a very messy situation." Morgan was looking at him intently, to see how he would react. Masha broke in again.

"Come off it, boys," she said. "Both of us saw you. We were there in the dark. One of you said Russian women were heavy. Feet were sticking out of the bag, and a slipper dropped off. It must have got pushed under a chair. We only found it when we were cleaning next morning. Didn't you notice the brown stains just now? That was fresh blood at the time. We could have gone to

214 *Mother Russia*

the police, but it wasn't any business of ours. We decided to wait and have a little word with you... When the time came." She smiled suddenly.

"No one's perfect," said Dasha.

"We're not going to rush off to the police just like that, are we?" said Masha. "Come on, tell us what really happened. Who killed her?"

"Well, we didn't," said Morgan quickly.

"No, no," said Llew shaking his head. He lowered his voice. "We never done anything like that. It was... *somebody else.*"

"Ivan?" said Masha. The men did not answer her directly.

"He just asked us to move this thing in a plastic bag," said Llew. "We thought it was a body straight away, mind. When we asked him later he said it was this girl Anna, one of his. He said she had a heart attack and died when she was being rogered by the Mayor of Porthcawl. It was to be all hush-hush, nobody in the borough wanted a scandal. Especially his wife."

"You didn't believe that, did you?" said Masha.

"Why not?" said Morgan. "Everybody knew he was one of the randiest men on the coast. This girl was Russian, and didn't have any relatives, so no one would know she died. It was her own fault, mind. If her heart was bad she should never have gone on to the game. It can cause embarrassment."

"So Ivan only wanted to get rid of her body without any fuss," said Llew. "No harm in that, is there? He was going to keep it in the fridge until he decided what to do with it. But when the kitchen caught fire, he was afraid the fridge might be opened."

Chapter Seven **215**

"I told you we should have gone back and looked for that fucking shoe when we was there," Morgan hissed to his companion. "It's evidence, isn't it?"

"Just a minute, boys," said Dasha, rather unexpectedly, "I've got to go to the ladies."

A little surprised at the suddenness of the announcement, the two men stopped speaking: perhaps she had eaten something that upset her. But off she went, taking the envelope with her, and leaving the three to enjoy their own company. Masha sipped her gin and tonic in a calm and composed manner.

"So you don't deny that you carried the body," she said. "If the police ever question you, it will be up to you to prove that you didn't kill her, that is, if the Porthcawl story was a lie. Have you seen yesterday's *Evening Post*? They've found her body, all cut up with no head, and with the other slipper on one of the feet. In a sewer down Penclawdd. And another body with it, too. Who dumped them, I wonder?"

Llew swallowed, Morgan froze, and the two men again looked at one another in utter alarm.

"Oh, don't worry," said Masha, with a sudden air of reassurance. "You're not in prison yet!"

"We haven't done nothing wrong," whined Llew, "only carry some bags. If you thought you saw us carrying a corpse, why didn't you go to the police and report us? Because they wouldn't believe you."

"We didn't go to the police because..." Masha paused to lend greater emphasis to her words, "because *we wanted to help you*. But let's wait until Dasha gets back, she may have something more to say."

"That'll be great," said Llew. There was another silence, this time longer.

216   *Mother Russia*

"She's a long time gone, though, isn't she?" said Morgan.

"She had to go to the bank," said Masha. "They're a bit slow at times."

"The bank?" said Llew, puzzled. "I thought she was going to the ladies'."

"No, the bank, really," said Masha. "We've hired a strong box there."

"Why is that?"

"To keep the slipper in. You see, it's got your fingerprints on it now! It could be vital evidence."

"Our fingerprints," said Llew, aghast. "We never saw it before! They can't pin anything on us."

"Oh, yes they can," said Masha, with a dangerous leer, "if they get hold of the shoe. But there's the tape as well. My sister had a pocket recorder pinned under her blouse, and we've recorded everything you said."

"Oh, Jesus!" cried Morgan, almost in tears. "What did we say?"

"All that was needed to get you into prison, boys, if the police ever find out, that is. You said you knew it was a body. And your fingerprints are on the shoe. You'd be prime suspects. But don't worry. It'll all be safe and sound in the bank vault. No one can get at it, except Dasha and me."

"Oh Gawd, I don't like it," said Morgan, with a very nasty expression indeed. "I don't like it at all."

"In other circumstances, anyone who done that to us..." Llew began.

Chapter Seven **217**

"Oh, I told you, don't worry," Masha insisted. "And you don't know the half of it yet. Let's wait for Dasha. She's got a nice proposition. Perhaps we can solve it."

Indeed, nothing more was said for a while: but a business-like expression lingered on Masha's face, and success gleamed in her eye. Her guests looked grey and crestfallen. It was clear that their normal desire to get drunk had deserted them completely.

"Oh, here she comes," said Masha, at last. And to her sister: "Did they take it, dear?"

"Yes, of course, no problem," said Dasha. "You've told the boys, have you?"

"Not everything. I thought I'd leave the proposition to you."

"Yes, boys," said Dasha. "We've got a good proposition for you."

"What is it?" said Llew, as a dreadful suspicion formed in his mind."

"To marry us, of course," cried Dasha. "It would be a double wedding with an Orthodox blessing!"

"My Gawd!" gasped Llew.

"And a nice party at Mother Russia to follow. There are lots of people we could invite."

"It couldn't be in church," said Masha, regretfully. "Not at our age. I don't know, though. Why not? Father Varfolomei would be very pleased. Perhaps Mr Whopp and Mr Alberthwaite could come as witnesses."

"Marriage?" said Morgan, incredulously. "That's what you've been getting at all the time, I can see it now. But we're only twenty four, both of us! We're too young for you!"

218   *Mother Russia*

"Well, there's no problem, is there?" said Dasha. "You're not under-age."

Suddenly Masha's face assumed its earnest expression. She was a business woman again.

"You'll get a wonderful deal, boys," she said. "We can offer you a share in Mother Russia when it re-opens. A partnership."

"We haven't got any money!"

"Well," said Masha, "we could offer you free lodging upstairs. And..." She paused meaningfully. "Free booze – that is, when we make a profit. What do you think of that?"

"There's a catch in it somewhere," said Morgan, obviously interested. "Free booze for life. But what do you get out of it, I mean at your age?"

"Young husbands, residence permits, and help in the restaurant," cried Dasha. "We'll be secure in Britain for life. Otherwise we'll find ourselves back in Verkhoyansk."

"But we hardly know you!" said Llew.

"Don't worry about a little thing like that," said Masha. "Remember, we'll be saving you from prison. We'll keep our mouths shut. And if necessary, we'll back you up against the police. If they think we're getting married, they'll probably keep off anyway."

"And if you find you don't like living with us, you can divorce us later," said Dasha generously. "As long as we've got residence permits. We can all go on a lovely honeymoon to Russia."

"Oh really?"

At that moment, as though by a stroke of fate, a couple of police officers came into the bar, and having perused

Chapter Seven **219**

the clientele, went out again. Evidently they were looking for someone; but in any case, the effect was unnerving.

"Well, er, it's a bit of a surprise like, just getting proposals of marriage in a pub," said Llew.

"From women who are old enough to be our aunties," added Morgan. "It would be a shock for my family. By the looks of it, my mother's younger than both of you."

"I might go for it if it's straightforward, like," said Llew, "with accommodation and free beer for life. I've got to get out of my place anyway. I'm behind with the rent."

"Free booze for life," said Morgan thoughtfully.

"Is the answer YES, then?" said Masha imperiously. "If not, we go to the police."

"What do you think, Llew?" asked Morgan.

"Well, yes, I suppose... We haven't got much choice, have we? But any wedding will have to be very, very quiet. So that no one would know. Otherwise we'll be the laughing stock of the whole bloody town."

"What about the evidence in the bank?" said Morgan. "We'll have to have it back."

"Of course," said Dasha, "when everything's nicely settled and we're married. And we've got our residence permits."

"Right," said Masha. "We were always taught to be very discreet in Russia. It's usually best to keep your mouth shut! So we've got a deal."

"You win," said Llew, looking at his glass.

"Drink up," said Masha. "There's plenty more where that came from. Now listen. When were you supposed to be seeing Ivan again?"

"This evening at Mother Russia. He has some jobs for us."

"*Keep away* from the restaurant this evening," said Masha earnestly. "The police are after Ivan, because they think he's behind the Penclawdd sewer murders. They're hoping to pick him up when he comes to open his fridge. They think there may be evidence inside it."

"How do you know that?" asked Llew.

"Olga and Trevor were called in for questioning this afternoon," said Dasha. "They told us. Whatever you do, keep away from Mother Russia tonight!"

"Ivan is mad, mad," said Llew. "He'll chop anything up. Even the Ukrainians are afraid of him. But don't worry, we'll steer clear."

And so, in the course of a few minutes, two marriages had apparently been arranged - and two tough young guys sheltered from justice.

The sea-gulls had long since perched for the night on their rocky promontories around Mumbles, but the few starlings which still fluttered through the evening air above Salubrious Passage would have noted, in their avian manner, a little activity in the back yard of Mother Russia. One of the old women, who worked there, her head wreathed in a kerchief, had thrown out a few scraps of food for their benefit, as usual. She had looked up to see whether any of them were around, before going back in. "Things are much safer now that Petya has disappeared," the starlings may well have thought, swooping down for closer inspection.

And finding no immediate danger, they landed, and hopped around, looking for the tastiest morsels available.

Chapter Seven **221**

A kitchen window was open, and the sound of voices could be heard. Since the birds could not understand what was being said inside, they pecked away, heedlessly. In fact Trevor, Olga and the two aunts were engaged in earnest consideration of imminent events. The tension, once more, was palpable.

"What time will Ivan be coming, then?" Dasha was saying.

"About six," said Trevor. "He had to get something from the fridge. Llew and Morgan were supposed to meet him here. Then they were going off somewhere together."

"Perhaps the boys won't come after all," said Masha. "Ouch!"

"Why did you step on her foot?" asked Trevor, who had seen it happen before. The two of them were evidently up to something again, but no matter.

"An accident," said Dasha. "Wasn't it, dear?"

"Well, we'd better get some tea and snacks ready for them," said Olga. "They've drunk most of the alcohol we had in stock. Oh, my God, I'm scared."

"Don't worry," said Trevor. "Everything will be okay."

"When are the police due?" asked Masha.

"At least an hour before Ivan arrives," answered Trevor. He looked at his watch. "Well, that means they'll be here soon. In plain clothes, I imagine."

"Of course," said Olga. "Oh, Trevor! What's going to happen next? It's just one nightmare after another."

"I told you, don't worry," he answered, giving her arm a little squeeze. She looked at him, glad to have him close by. But her apprehension was catching. The aunts looked at one another uneasily, and Dasha started to wail. "Oh,

222   *Mother Russia*

I'm frightened, too. That Ivan can do anything. He'll kill us all."

Masha looked at her in tearful agreement.

"Don't be ridiculous," said Trevor. "We'll have half a dozen hefty policemen here."

At that moment the doorbell rang.

"That must be them," said Olga. "I'll go and open it!"

The three people in the kitchen listened intently as Olga undid the latch. A man's voice could be heard. Oh horrors! It was Ivan: he had come early.

"Oh, hullo, Ivan Ivanovich," they heard Olga say. "I thought you would be coming a little later."

Ivan appeared not to hear her.

"Have Llew and Morgan come?" He sounded a little drunk. "We were supposed to meet here."

"Not yet," said Olga.

"Oh, my God," Dasha whispered. "What can we do? An uninvited guest..."

But Olga was already leading the guest into the kitchen. As he came through the door everyone was struck by his manner. Not only was he slightly drunk: but he seemed to be on edge, aggressive, and exuded an evil potency which had not been apparent before. He kept looking around, as though expecting someone to be following him.

"I really think he's mad," Trevor thought to himself. "But I wonder whether he suspects something?"

"Have a glass of tea while you're waiting, Ivan Ivanovich," Olga said.

"Tea?" he said. "Isn't there any vodka?" He sat down as Dasha obediently went to the cupboard to get a forlorn bottle. Ivan was not, however, destined to imbibe, for no sooner had he sat down than the doorbell rang again.

"It must be Llew and Morgan," said Ivan, pouring himself a large measure. "Open it, somebody."

Trevor left the kitchen. He had but one thought in mind: was it the police? Had they lost the advantage of surprise? It looked as though the ambush was going badly wrong.

Indeed it was: events were occurring in the wrong order. Outside, in Salubrious Passage, half a dozen heavily-built gentlemen in plain clothes emerged from a couple of unmarked cars. It was the expected contingent from the cop-shop with the Inspector and Constable, whom we have already met, amongst them. They had all come a little later than planned because (had Inspector Watkins dared to admit it) he and Constable Moss had tarried over an extra game of draughts.

"Well, boys," said the Inspector, as they gathered around him. "We're a bit behind time, but no matter. Now you know the plan: we go inside, take up suitable concealed positions in the restaurant and kitchen (making sure all the exits are covered.) When this Ivan Kravchenko rings the doorbell Mrs. Morozova will answer it and let him in. With any luck he'll open the fridge himself, but he should have the keys in his pocket anyway. We jump out and arrest him in the name of the law."

"But we haven't got anything on him yet, have we?"

Inspector Watts was obviously somewhat irritated.

"He's wanted for questioning, isn't he? And there may be something of interest in that fridge. It sounds highly suspicious to me."

"But what about accomplices?" asked Constable Moss. "He might not come alone."

"Why do you think there are eight of us?" answered the Inspector. "No problem. We can arrest Ivan and any other bugger with him, in like manner." The Inspector liked to slip an occasional expletive into his speech. "Now lads, be very civil to the people inside – they're helping us. There's Mrs. Morozova, Olga, Trevor Jenkins, and two old aunts, quite harmless creatures, so we don't want them frightened. Everything clear? Quietly now."

He led his men down the Passage to the restaurant, and rang the bell. It was opened almost immediately by Trevor, wide-eyed: "He's come already," he mouthed, just loud enough for them to hear. Then he stood aside as they tip-toed in.

"And how have things been going, Ivan Ivanovich?" Olga was saying, back in the kitchen, in a brave attempt at light conversation. "Good cockling weather?"

"Not very," said Ivan, glancing expectantly at the doorway. "I'm having a bit of trouble with the business. It isn't easy to make an honest living these days. There's a lot of competition, people poking and prying..." He stopped speaking, sensing that someone had come into the premises: but there was no murmur of voices, as one might expect. "Who is it?" he said.

At that very moment the kitchen door was thrown open and Inspector Watkins, followed by Constable Moss, the plain clothes men, and Trevor burst in. Ivan jumped up.

Chapter Seven **225**

"I arrest you, Ivan Kravchenko, on suspicion..." the Inspector began dramatically. It was one of his favourite phrases, uttered at a few cherished moments in his police career.

"Oh no you don't," said Ivan Ivanovich, as though, somehow, he had been expecting trouble. With a sudden darting movement he slipped behind Olga and seized her, his left arm firmly under her diplomas: with his right he drew a razor from his inside jacket pocket and rested the edge, feather-light, against Olga's throat.

"Stand back, everyone!" he shouted. "Don't touch me!"

Everybody in the kitchen froze, as though making a charade tableau. It was clear that any struggle could have appalling consequences.

"Let her go immediately," said Inspector Watkins.

Ivan did not answer, but looked around in desperation. A single thought flashed through everyone's mind – "He's mad, mad! He can never get away with it!" But Ivan was edging towards the back door, pulling Olga with him, keeping everyone else in front of him. Trevor, though, had unobtrusively grasped an iron saucepan – just in case there was any chance to intervene. It seemed that any voluntary submission on Ivan's part was out of the question. Obviously, the Russian hoped to tough it out and make a getaway, using Olga as a hostage.

At this point, Constable Moss, who had done a special three-day course in handling hostage-takers, saw an admirable chance of using his new-found skills.

"It's all right, Ivan, sir," he said, soothingly. "Take it easy. Don't do anything silly. You can't get away. Let's have a little talk about things. I'm sure we can find a solution."

Ivan, for a brief moment, seemed interested. But Olga, sensing that he was listening to the Constable, tried to jerk herself free, and Ivan tightened his grip again. So much for the hostage-taking course, thought the Inspector. I knew it was a bloody waste of time.

"Do as I say," Ivan growled to Olga, "or you'll be a corpse, too. Come with me." Slowly he made his way backwards, towards the back door, pulling her with him.

"You haven't got a chance," Inspector Watkins called out. "We've got the area surrounded. Give yourself up to avoid further charges!"

But Ivan appeared to take no notice, he was desperate, and not a little drunk.

As we all know, dear reader, fate is a strange thing: it may intrude at any place or time, and take the most unexpected forms. Both of the aunts, as it happened, suffered from an abdominal condition known as diverticulitis, one consequence of which is a tendency to inordinate flatulence. And under the dreadful tension of that moment, when poor Olga could have been murdered before their very eyes, one of the old ladies – I shall not reveal which – lost control of her wind and – to put it crudely – farted. And very expressively.

Of course everyone heard it: farting is just as laughable – or socially heinous an act – in Russia as in other lands, and attracts no less attention, especially in attentive company. The communist regime did nothing to change that perception, and Lenin himself was rumoured to have been a frequent offender. It would be of interest to psychologists to note that even a hardened criminal like Ivan, in perilous circumstances, could be distracted by so minor a social misdemeanour.

Chapter Seven **227**

Be all that as it may, the Russian seemed to relax his guard just for an instant, a fraction of a second. But it was enough for Trevor to raise his saucepan and bring it down with all his might on the Ivan's Slavonic pate. The Russian sank to the floor, unconscious, and Olga jumped to freedom.

"Handcuff him!" cried the Inspector. "But check he's all right!"

In fact Ivan was already stirring, much to Trevor's relief – facing a police charge of manslaughter did not fit into his immediate plans.

"Lift him onto this chair, will you," the Inspector told some of the men, "and get some cuffs on him. Call an ambulance, Moss. They'll probably have to do an X-ray of the skull, just routine. Now who farted? That act of flatulence changed the whole situation, and may have saved a human life. It's a key issue in the case, and will go into my report. A police officer has to be meticulous about these things. And there may be a big reward for the criminal's capture in Russia."

"It was me," said Dasha, quickly.

"No, it was me," Masha insisted. "I've had an upset stomach, and I've been doing it all day."

"Don't try and pull that one on me," her sister responded, looking around for a spare saucepan, while her sister did the same. "You liar! You'd say anything to get a reward!"

They were obviously rearing for a fight.

"For God's sake," said Olga, who had somewhat recovered her composure, "you aren't going to fight over *that*, are you? Trevor is the hero of the moment, he's the one who really saved me!"

228   *Mother Russia*

"Right," cried the Inspector, turning to some of his underlings. "Restrain these two old ladies, will you? Keep them well apart. In addition to two murders and attempted armed abduction, we've got a serious assault case on our hands. Constable, arrest Trevor Jenkins, will you?"

Trevor went pale.

"My God!" he said. "What for?"

"I am charging you with common assault occasioning actual bodily harm," said the Inspector. "You could have killed that poor man. Constable, handcuff Jenkins as well, will you? We may decide to release you after interrogation," said the Inspector, turning to the culprit, "but it will depend on how things go. You can't go round bashing people on the head with iron saucepans, you know. And in due course Mr. Kravchenko here may wish to sue you for assault, whether he is in prison or not. How would *you* like it? Mind, perhaps you could plead extenuating circumstances. It will all have to be sorted out. You'll be allowed a solicitor."

At that moment there was a sigh and a heavy thump as Olga collapsed on the floor.

"Oh, Heavens, now she's fainted as well," said Constable Moss.

The two aunts rushed over and started patting her cheeks. Trevor shook himself free from the grasp of one of the plain-clothes men and joined them. He kneeled down and cradled her head in his arm.

"It's all your fault," Masha screeched, looking accusingly at the Inspector.

"Where am I, where am I," said Ivan, weakly.

Chapter Seven   **229**

"You're being arrested for attempted murder," the Inspector explained.

The Russian just stared at him dully. Olga was coming to as well.

"I never thought things would turn out like this," she said in a scarcely audible voice. "Now they've arrested you, Trevor, and you haven't done anything wrong!"

She struggled to her feet. "You aren't having him," she shouted tearfully. "He hasn't done anything wrong. He saved my life!" Two policemen tried to restrain her, but she managed to thrust them aside.

"Let Trevor go!" she yelled, and kicked the nearest one on the shin. The unfortunate officer hopped about in pain.

"Grab her," said the Inspector. "We can't have this, either. We'll charge her with using violence against a police officer and obstructing the police in the performance of their duties."

"She's got a hell of a kick in her, too," said the policeman.

Meanwhile Masha and Dasha looked on in agonised astonishment.

"You can't arrest innocent people, either," Masha screeched. "Trevor and Olga were helping you. It's just like Russia."

"All police actions are carefully considered," said the Inspector.

Masha sidled up to him and took him by the elbow. "Come over here... Let's do a deal, like in Russia. Take a bottle of vodka and let them go. I've got one hidden away."

230 *Mother Russia*

The Inspector graced her with an icy smile.

"Be careful, madam," he declared, "or you may be arrested, too."

"What for?"

"Attempted bribery... Now let's see," the inspector added, looking around. "Yes, the fridge. Why has it got a padlock on it? I never seen a fridge with a padlock. Is this the one that belongs to Kravchenko?"

"Yes," said Olga. "We've got nothing to do with it. We haven't even got a key."

"There may be one in his pocket."

The owner of the required object was still sitting in a daze.

"Moss," said the Inspector, "frisk him, will you?"

The Constable bent over the reclining figure, and in a moment or two had produced a bunch of keys. "Perhaps it's one of these, sir!"

Inspector Watkins took them, and, after a little fiddling, found one which indeed fitted the lock. He removed the lock from its hasp and flung the fridge door open. Everyone gasped.

Apart from fish, tins of caviar, and what looked like a small pile of trays, there, on the top shelf, but half concealed in bloodstained plastic bags, were two battered human heads, cut off at the neck. The plain white flesh contrasted vividly with dried blood stains on the temples and cheeks, and the dark green insignia of bags from one of London's most prestigious shops – Fortnum and Mason's, in Piccadilly...

Chapter Seven **231**

Olga fainted again and the two old ladies grasped one another for support. Tough though they were, they had never seen anything like it, not even in Russia.

"Ah-ha!" said Inspector Watkins, with a hugely satisfied look. "So we've found them after all. I can guess where they came from, these. From whose shoulders, I mean ... That's another step in solving the Penclawdd sewer mystery; we could hardly get anywhere without the heads. They were probably severed to impede identification of the other parts. The whole thing is coming together!"

"Ho, ho, coming together, that's rich, isn't it?" said Constable Moss. "The heads and the shoulders." And then, in an attempt at macabre humour: "They'll use an industrial glue, I expect."

"The people involved must have been rather choosey about their groceries, mind," the Inspector continued. "Fortnum and Mason's is an expensive shop in Piccadilly. I went there with the missus when we was in London. Constable, get a couple of those wine glasses trays (he gestured towards a shelf) and put the heads on them, will you? Pick them up careful, now, by the ears, just using a couple of fingers. We don't want your dabs all over them! The forensic boys will have a field day. We've got to be sure the heads fit the shoulders!"

"I've never picked up severed heads, Inspector," said Constable Moss, hesitantly. "I don't feel well."

"Nonsense!" said Inspector Watkins. "And you a serving officer! What about your family butcher? He's cutting meat every day of the week, isn't he! Got the trays?" The Constable gingerly did as he was told. "Okay, set them aside for a moment. We've got to do a full inventory of everything that's in this fridge." He pulled out a notebook. "Check these with me, will you?"

232 *Mother Russia*

"Two human heads, one male, one female, with dried blood, in Fortnum and Mason's plastic bags.

"Three large round tins with Russian lettering, oh yes, English as well. It's caviar."

"Must be worth quite a bit, that," said the Constable. "I've never had the proper stuff. You can buy a cheap kind."

"I had some once," said Inspector Watkins. "We had a visiting delegation from the Russian militia."

"What does it taste like?

The inspector paused. "Well... fishy. A bit like laverbread, really... Next, two large sturgeon... Now what are those?"

His gaze fell on a stack of what appeared to be small wooden trays, decorated.

"Let's have a gander." He lifted the top one: one side of it had been painted with what looked like a religious image, heavily varnished.

He carried it over to the window, so as to see it better.

"Icons!" said the inspector. "We'll have to have these assessed by an expert. They may be valuable antiques. Perhaps stolen." His eyes lit up: if it was a big haul, promotion might be in the offing. "Wait a minute, though. There's something peculiar..."

The constable peered over his shoulder. "Inspector!" he cried. "Look at them tits! I've never seen an icon with naked tits. And painted blue."

"You're right, Constable," said the Inspector. "Big ones, too... Lewd Icons. Blasphemy. Possibly a vicious line in pornography. I've never heard of this. It may be illegal, if minors have access. My God, what a case!"

Chapter Seven **233**

"All of this stuff belongs to Ivan Ivanovich," said Olga. "We suspected he was using his fridge to store things."

"Storing pornography is not a punishable offence," said the inspector, in false, fair-minded tones. "It's what happens to it after that matters."

"Perverting minors after Sunday school," said Trevor ironically.

"Perverting minors is a serious offence," said the inspector, "inside Sunday school or out."

"I think they must have been for smuggling back into Russia," said Trevor, helpfully. "We had two Russian Orthodox priests around; they knew about a trade in lewd icons, and they were very upset. Of course, we had no idea that Ivan was involved."

"So the Russian Orthodox Church is mixed up in it as well!" said Constable Moss. "It gets messier and messier, doesn't it?"

The Inspector viewed the scene and suppressed another smile. He couldn't believe his luck: "What a selection – murder, decapitated bodies, razor attacks, suspicious foreign nationals, and now a new kind of pornography!"

"Right, stick them icons back where they came from," he said, "but don't scratch them. They'll be needed as evidence in due course. And the caviar. We'd better get back to the station with the three suspects, we'll have to consider whether to bring charges against them." He paused for a moment, looking at Masha and Dasha. "Should he hustle them in as well?" he thought. "For attempted bribery?" Then he remembered his own ageing aunties Florry and Dossy in Tonypandy. Well, perhaps not yet.

"You two ladies can stay here," he declared, "but I would like you to give the constable your particulars. You won't be going anywhere in the next few days, will you? We may require to call you in for interview at the station. And meanwhile we'll keep the keys to the fridge."

Masha and Dasha exchanged glances: would they have to show their passports? Fortunately the police, at that moment, were too busy to ask for them, and the immediate danger passed. Ivan was now back on his feet, and the three detainees – he, Trevor, and Olga – were hustled into a police van which drew up outside.

At last the door closed behind them, leaving Masha and Dasha alone in the kitchen. The clock ticked loudly in the corner. A little traffic could be heard in the distance. After all the commotion, the silence seemed strange indeed.

"What an evening," said Dasha. "I can't remember anything like it since dad had that fight with Rasputin. Remember? The militia came and arrested everyone. Good job I farted. It changed the whole situation."

"It's said that just before Ivan the Terrible killed his own son, in a fit of rage, he farted audibly," said Dasha. "Some of the noble Boyars heard him, but they were so taken aback that they didn't intervene to save the boy. If it hadn't been for that fart, his son would have lived, and probably become tsar of Russia. The whole history of the land would have been changed. I read it in Klyuchevsky."

"I never heard that before," said Masha. "But I was never very good at history."

Epilogue

(All loose ends tied up ....)

CELEBRATIONS IN SALUBRIOUS PASSAGE

by Gloria Evans
(*EVENING POST* REPORTER)

Salubrious Passage, at the bottom of Wind Street, is well known to most, if not all the inhabitants of our town. The traditional explanation for the intriguing name was that in olden times the passage was used as an escape route for young men fleeing press gangs and arduous service in the Royal Navy. More recently, however, the passage has become famous as the location of one of Swansea's more exotic eateries – Mother Russia – which specialises in tasty dishes from Eastern Slavdom, not to mention a fortune-telling booth, and a massage parlour!

Readers of the *Evening Post* will be delighted to learn that on Saturday last the restaurant was re-opened, following an unfortunate fire which all but destroyed the fine kitchens some months ago. The gala re-opening was enhanced by a private celebration of what were surely Swansea's most unusual nuptuals in living memory. Two mature Russian ladies (age irrelevant), the sisters Maria and Daria Morozova, who produced the delicious fare, were earlier in the day betrothed to two local Welsh boys, Llewellyn and Morgan Thomas, both of Mansel Street, Brynhyfred. The re-opening had been preceded by a small Russian marriage ceremony at Caersalem

Chapel, with a Russian Orthodox priest, Father Varfolomei, officiating. Both the ladies were from the distant Siberian town of Verkhoyansk. The four newly-weds looked forward to many long and happy years in our community.

And not only that!

Mother Russia is owned jointly by Trevor Lewis, a Hafod boy, and Miss Olga Morozova, the brides' niece, also from Verkhoyansk.

Did we glimpse them holding hands behind the samovar?

Indeed we did! And beaming with pleasure, they told your reporter that they were delighted to announce their own engagement, with the Happy Day to follow some time in the spring.

Among the Russians and distinguished guests at the reception were Mr. Algernon Alberthwaite, Swansea Council's newly appointed Chief Inspector of Environmental Health, and Inspector Paul Watkins of Swansea police.

Mr. Alberthwaite congratulated the owners on the restoration of the kitchen facilities, and revealed that his department had been able to make a small discretionary grant to restore (as Mr. Alberthwaite put it) a unique culinary facility in our town.

Inspector Watkins, for his part, referred to the recent attempt by a notorious Russian gang-leader to make the restaurant a base for various criminal activities, not least a Russian call-girl ring. All of that story was duly reported in the *Evening Post*. The Inspector emphasised the bravery which both Olga and Trevor (and indeed the two brides) showed during the police apprehension of the principal Russian criminal involved. He is currently lodged in Swansea prison and the girls, mostly illegal immigrants, have been sent back to Russia. The case will shortly be coming up in a local court, so…

Watch this space..!

Printed in the United Kingdom
by Lightning Source UK Ltd.
133155UK00001B/10-51/P